FORGED IN MAGIC

DRAGON'S GIFT THE PROTECTOR BOOK 5

LINSEY HALL

For Carolyn, who has the biggest heart.

CHAPTER ONE

As a supernatural, I was used to the fantastic.

Sanaria, the main city in the Vampire Realm, took the cake, however. I'd only been here five minutes and I was already wowed. Ares and I had just parked his motorcycle on the outskirts of town and had walked onto the main street. I stopped on the sidewalk, taking it all in.

I whistled. "When you said there were no cars in the Vampire Realm, I wasn't expecting vampire horses pulling floating carriages."

They trotted down the street, fangs gleaming white in the moonlight. More bustled through the narrow road, each wearing a feathery headdress. Equine opera singers. The carriages were done up, too, bedecked with all different colors and a variety of trims.

Ares took my hand and pulled me along. "Come, the Illuminarium is waiting."

"Yeah, you're right."

We'd come here to meet with the Vampire Realm's institution of knowledge—not for me to gawk. After we'd saved Elesius from Drakon two days ago, we'd given the Illuminarium the power source that Drakon had used for his evil spell. They'd contacted us a couple hours ago, and I was crossing my fingers that they'd discovered something useful.

While I followed Ares, my attention was on the city around me. The buildings were four stories high, fabulously ornate structures built of white stone that reflected the moonlight, making the whole town glow. Street lamps full of lightning bugs gleamed golden and bright. Strands of fairy lights decorated the buildings and stretched high above the street. They were made of lightning bugs, too.

"Vampires like light," Ares said, clearly having noticed my interest.

"It's fabulous. But do the bugs like it?"

He laughed. "It's a spell, not real lightning bugs."

Whew.

We reached a busier street with more foot traffic, squeezing in on the crowded sidewalk. For the first time in my life, I was surrounded by vampires. They didn't come to the human realm often, so it was a bit disconcerting. Especially since some of them seemed to be looking at my neck. Ares might've been highly cautious about not drinking my blood, but were *they*?

I shivered, pressing closer to Ares. Only then did I realize that they were moving deferentially out of our way.

"They're impressed that you're the Enforcer, aren't they?" I asked.

He shrugged slightly. "Yes."

"That must be annoying. Is that why Doyen and Magisteria spend so much time hanging out alone at their thrones in the woods?"

"I believe so. Some things do not change quickly in the Vampire Realm. Not just the horses and carriages, but the awe of authority."

"That must be exhausting."

"It is."

A huge building loomed at the end of the street, reminding me of Buckingham Palace or the Taj Mahal—big, white, and fancy. But with a magical twist, as more of the firefly lights glittered around the top domes.

"That's the Illuminarium," Ares said.

"Impressive."

We sailed through the crowd, which parted like the Red Sea. When the Pūķi swooped out of the air to join us, their fiery red forms hovering above, people's gazes turned from curious to awed. And they were aimed right at me.

"Why are they looking at me like that?" I murmured.

"Not used to seeing the Pūķi, which are clearly following you."

Which made me special. That could be both good and bad, depending. Since my specialness was related to me defeating Drakon and saving the world's magic, I was going to go with sorta bad. It was a weight that I didn't want on my shoulders. But the only way to remove the weight was to succeed.

I hurried my pace, determined to make use of every minute we had. With Drakon always a step ahead of us, I needed to use my time wisely.

The Illuminarium loomed overhead as we approached. The road led right up to the gate.

The intricately twisted wrought iron was beautiful, forming swoops and swirls that would keep out intruders while impressing the hell out of them. Beyond, fountains shot out of the ground, synchronized jets of water that glinted in the moonlight. A hundred yards away, the white building gleamed.

"Your culture idolizes knowledge," I said.

"Yes. It's the best way to ensure a safe and happy life."

"How do we get in?"

"This way." Ares pressed his hand to the iron gate. Magic glowed, then the gate swung open.

Power sparkled across my skin as we stepped through the

wide opening. I couldn't quite pinpoint it, but it was both eerie and nice at the same time.

A row of fountains led straight to the building fifty yards away. Hundreds of jets of water shot up and splashed down. Between them, shadowy white figures drifted. Almost like ghosts in robes.

"What are they?" I whispered.

"Memories of knowledge," Ares said. "They are what help give this place its magic."

They ignored us as if we weren't here, hundreds of them. "Why wasn't I able to see them before?"

"They've chosen to reveal themselves. It's a good sign." He glanced down at me. "Not everyone is permitted entrance to the Illuminarium."

"Why?"

He shrugged. "Not everyone is worthy."

We passed by the ghosts and the fountains, finally reaching the massive steps that led up to the entrance. The architecture was so odd—a combination of many styles. Ancient Greek, Northern European, Indian. As if the builder had taken his favorite styles and smashed them all together.

We climbed the stairs. Huge wooden doors swung open, permitting us entrance to a round room built entirely of white stone.

"They sure do like their white here," I murmured.

Ares chuckled.

In the middle of the room, a basin of water sat on a pedestal. There was nothing else. Not even a door. It was deadly silent.

"Where's the door?"

"I don't know." Ares inspected the space. "This room changes for everyone who enters."

I walked around the perimeter, searching for a hidden exit. After a few minutes, it was clear that there was none. "No one is coming to greet us, are they?"

"It doesn't seem that way."

I shivered, the energy in the air making my skin prickle. It was almost expectant. As if we were being watched.

I turned back toward the center of the room. Ares stood next to the fountain in the middle, gazing into the depths.

I stepped toward him, and the room went black.

My hair stood on end. "Ares?"

No response.

"Ares!"

Silence.

Heart pounding, I called upon my magic, envisioning a torch. But none appeared in my hand. My conjuring wasn't working. I tried again, forcing all of my power into creating a torch. Or a weapon.

Nothing.

My magic was dead inside me, like the ghosts out in the courtyard.

Real fear swept through me, chilling my skin. I reached out, stumbling forward. "Ares!"

Silence.

He really wasn't there.

My heartbeat thundered in my ears, nearly drowning out the sound of lapping waves.

Lapping waves? There was water here?

The sound came from all around. I squinted into the pitch black, desperate to see.

There was nothing but blackness and the sound of the water. Slowly, I walked forward, arms outstretched.

My foot splashed against water. My throat tightened, making it hard to breathe. From the lapping of the waves, it sounded like I was surrounded. I bent, dipping my fingertips into the water. The scent of sulfur tickled my nose as pain sliced through my hand.

"Ah!" I jerked my hand back, shaking it and panting hard. The burn was like acid, eating away at the tips of my fingers. Tears prickled my eyes.

Holy shit. I was surrounded by an acid sea.

I'd only ever heard of such things.

I stumbled back from the water, mind racing. Again, I tried to conjure a torch or a light. But nothing happened.

There was a reason for this. It wasn't random. And there would be a way out.

I would find it.

I dragged in a ragged breath, forcing my mind to calm. What had Ares said about this place? That not everyone was permitted to enter here and that the place changed depending on the person.

Me.

And it stopped me from using my magic.

Which made it a test. But of what? Not of my power or my magical strength.

Something else, then.

A sharp cry rent the air.

A baby.

I spun, frantic, but could see nothing. The cry came again, the loud squall of a baby in distress. A really young baby.

My heart thundered as thoughts raced through my head.

The cry came again, sharper and higher. To my left. Not far. Danger pricked on the air, a threat so strong that it stung my skin. I couldn't tell what it was, but it was going for the child.

I raced toward the cry, my boots splashing into the acid sea. How long would the leather protect me? Would I have to swim to the baby? Could I even survive that?

The cry—sharper now. I gritted my teeth and stepped deeper into the water.

A warm red light glowed, temporarily blinding me. I blinked. The room was lit with red light, enough for me to see that there was a stone path through the acid sea, just to my left. Near it, a bassinet floated on the water, like something from myth or legend. All around, the sea stretched out, tiny ripples breaking the surface. The room had no more walls, and the patch of land upon which I stood was the size of my living room.

Overhead, the Pūķi fluttered, their glowing scarlet bodies providing the light.

"Thank you." My voice was desperate, tinged with tears.

I raced for the pathway made of stones jutting from the water. Quickly, I leapt across, heading for the bassinet. It looked to be sinking, slowly dipping deeper into the water as the acid cut into the wicker.

The squalling of the child chilled my skin. I moved faster, teetering on the stones as my haste made me clumsy.

Panting, I reached the bassinet, grabbing the handle and swooping it up. The pale red light of the Pūķi illuminated the interior of the bassinet.

Empty.

The crying stopped.

My shoulders sagged.

Definitely a test, then.

All that fear for nothing. I almost tossed the bassinet back into the sea, but then clutched it to my chest. That seemed disrespectful, and in all the ancient tasks, disrespect was punished.

Holding the bassinet, I spun in a circle, balancing on my rock, muscles straining from tension.

"Where next?" I asked the Pūķi. The stone path led into the distance in one direction and back to shore in the other. I had to choose.

The Pūķi had nothing to say. Instead, they fluttered overhead, dragon lanterns that kept me from plunging to a terrible death.

"Since I know where I've been, I might as well go somewhere new."

With the bassinet clutched to my side, I turned and hopped across the stones that led into the blackness.

"Ares!" I called.

No response, just the lapping of the waves against the rocks upon which I stood. Worry tightened in my chest, but I forced it away. It wouldn't help me finish this. And Ares could take care of himself—I had faith in that. This was probably just a test for me, anyway.

Finally, I caught sight of land just ahead. Flat and rocky, just like where I'd come from. Except that my stone pathway stopped about ten feet short of the shore.

I couldn't jump that.

I swallowed hard, looking around for anything to help.

Nothing caught my eye. Just the acid sea and the far shore. The bassinet dragged at my arm, suddenly heavier. I look inside. A coiled rope had appeared.

I grinned. Good thing I hadn't chucked the bassinet into the sea.

Though I had no idea what to do with it, I withdrew the rope. The prickly hemp scratched my palms.

The rope writhed and shifted, turning into a snake with glinting green scales. A small shriek escaped me just as the snake leapt from my hands.

I swore it had grinned at me, fangs shining in the light.

It plunged into the acid sea, then raced for shore, cutting through the water like a great anaconda. It grew as it swam, stretching between the shore and the stone I stood upon.

When it reached the bank, it stopped. The tail was at my feet, flicking on the stone.

"Oh fates." I swallowed hard, studying the snake.

His body grew wider and flatter. A bridge?

When he turned his head back to look at me, the invitation was clear in his gleaming black eyes.

"Are you serious?" I asked the snake.

He didn't really nod, but it looked like he smiled. Could snakes even smile?

I took it to be a yes and tentatively moved a foot toward his back. I pressed down with a bit of weight, heart thudding in my ears. When his back didn't bow and he didn't slither away, a weak laugh escaped me.

"All right, then. I think I'm in a weird fairytale." I stepped on the snake's back fully.

I hesitated just briefly, awed at the insane circumstance—I mean, I was used to weird magic but a friendly snake bridge?— then I raced across, balancing on the back of my new friend.

I leapt over his head, landing on solid ground. I laughed, sounding crazed to my own ears, then turned.

The snake was already shrinking and slithering away, not at all bothered by the acid.

"Thanks!" I called to his retreating back.

The Pūķi flew over to hover above my head. I looked up. "Have you ever seen anything like that?"

They just stared at me.

"I'll assume you agree with me." I turned to search the area where I stood. It was dark and barren, lit with the Pūķi's eerie red glow. "Onward." I clutched the bassinet and moved forward.

It wasn't long before a great big stone appeared in front of me. It was the size of an office desk. A sword stuck out of the top of it.

"You have got to be kidding me," I muttered.

The Pūķi fluttered down to sit on the ground near the stone. Their gazes riveted to the gleaming blade. I approached, studying the sword.

"That's my blade!" I cried.

I didn't care that I'd moved fully into talking-to-myself territory. This was too weird. That was the sword that Laima, the goddess of fate, had given me. How did it get here?

I reached out, gingerly touching the end of the pommel.

It didn't feel quite right. A replica of my blade.

"I guess this makes me Arthur." I peered into the bassinet at my side, just to see if another helpful thing would appear. Maybe a chatty baby would explain what the heck was going on.

But of course there was nothing in the bassinet.

So I set it on the ground and turned back to the sword. I rubbed my hands together and tried to think worthy thoughts. Things like helping old ladies across the street and cleaning up trash on the sidewalk.

I wrapped my hands around the hilt and propped my boot on the stone, then I yanked with all my might, giving it everything I had.

I flew backward, sword gripped tightly in my hand, and landed hard on my butt.

Pain flared through my tailbone, and tears popped to my eyes. Through the tears, the blade sparkled in the red light of the Pūķi's glow.

Damn. That had hurt. Probably should have tried with a little less force.

I climbed to my feet, aching.

This worthiness stuff was tough.

In front of me, the stone transformed into the white basin that had originally sat in the center of the room. The darkness receded, as did the acid sea. Light returned, the walls around me gleaming white.

I spun, searching for Ares.

He lay on his back at the side of the room.

"Ares!"

CHAPTER TWO

I raced for Ares's prone form and fell to my knees at his side. I shook his shoulder, my heart thundering. "Ares!"

He blinked blearily, sitting up.

I gripped his arm to help him. "Are you all right?"

"Yes." His voice was scratchy. A sparkly silver dust glittered on the front of his shirt. "I think I fell asleep."

I pointed to the dust. "Magic. Sleeping potion, maybe."

"Damn." He looked up at me, eyes now alert. "Are you all right?"

"Yeah. A little bit of excitement, but I'm fine."

"A challenge?" His gaze fell on the sword that I'd laid on the ground. "Did you have to pull that from a stone?"

"I did." I almost cracked a joke about the Illuminarium needing to come up with their own ideas, but the memory of the snake bridge stopped me. They had their own ideas. And a sense of humor, perhaps.

Ares stood, and I joined him, swooping down to pick up my blade.

"What happened to your hand?" He grabbed my wrist and raised my hand, studying my fingertips.

I winced at the sight of the skin there, reddened and eaten away from touching the acid sea. I couldn't see bone, but it was close. It still hurt, but not as badly. Because the nerves had been damaged?

"Part of the challenge," I said. "Mostly a mistake on my part."

"Come." Ares led me to the stone basin in the center of the room. Holding my injured hand, he dipped my fingertips into the clear liquid within.

It was thick, a viscous substance. Pain flared. I jerked my hand, but Ares held me firm.

"I'm sorry." Regret rang in his voice. "Your nerves are repairing themselves."

The pain faded. Through the clear liquid, I could see my fingertips turning less red and ragged. Finally, they were whole again. Ares withdrew my hand.

"How'd you know to do that?" I asked.

"I've made use of this basin myself." His gaze met mine, a sexy grin tugging at the corner of his mouth. "Did you meet the snake who forms a bridge?"

"I did!"

"Charles is a good sort," he said. "I've always liked him."

"Where did—"

A door opened in the wall, in a place where there had been no door at all. I snapped my mouth shut.

A cloaked figure entered. I could see no face and got no hint at gender. The sparkling white cloak draped gracefully to the floor, the hood concealing any features.

"Come." Ares waved me forward.

I followed him toward the figure, who waited patiently, silently, by the door. Tension prickled across my skin, and my heart thundered.

This was the figure who'd put me through the trials. Dangerous trials. I had to assume I'd passed, but that didn't mean I could trust someone who'd surrounded me with a sea of acid.

The figure inclined its head as we neared, then gestured toward the door with a sweep of his hand.

We entered a huge space, round and bright. A dome overhead glinted with a mosaic of rainbow tiles. Firefly lights sparkled above, making the tiles glitter with gemstone brilliance. I had to drag my gaze toward the rest of the room, which was all stark white. Bookshelves lined the walls, but every spine was white and blank.

In the middle of the room, a large round table stood. Built of white marble, it looked like a massive altar. Chairs surrounded it, each containing a cloaked figure.

Every single thing and person in here—besides the fabulous ceiling—was the color of snow. I'd almost missed seeing the people, they blended so well with their surroundings.

Magic signatures filled the room. The smell of ink, old paper, and leather binding. The feeling of paper beneath my fingertips and the little rush a breeze created when one flipped through the pages of a book. The feeling of satisfaction after having finished a good story.

Knowledge. These were the signatures of knowledge.

A large black gemstone sat in the middle of the table.

The magical battery.

As Ares and the original cloaked figure joined me, I could feel the scrutiny of those sitting around the table. It burned my skin. This felt like being on stage.

As a group, the thirteen individuals around the table lowered their hoods.

Their skin was the snow white of the marble table, but they had no real features. They had noses—sort of—and lips. Almost. The subtle topography of eyes. They looked like unfinished statues. Modern art.

A figure to my left rose gracefully, and spoke, the voice somewhere between a man's and a woman's. "You have done well,

Phoenix Knight, and proven yourself worthy of the information that we will pass on to you."

"Thank you."

"It is vital that this knowledge be protected and used well. The Pūķi appeared to you, lighting your way and proving your worthiness."

I hesitated to mention that I'd been friends with the Pūķi for a while now. Though they probably already knew a lot about me if they'd managed to create a replica of my sword.

"What did you learn about the battery?" I asked. "What is it made of?"

The figure sat, then stared at the stone. "Extensive tests have determined that it is a crystal of Synnaroe. Its magic is a gift from the gods, who each gave a part of their power to the stone so that their magic would live on even after they were long gone."

I frowned. "You said *a* crystal of Synnaroe. Are there more?"

"Yes. It is part of an ancient pair of crystals formed at the center of the earth and recovered by giants over three thousand years ago. They were separated long ago."

"Which means that the other battery Drakon seeks—it is the partner stone."

"It stands to reason, yes."

"Do these crystals have any connection with dragons?" Ares asked.

"Not to our knowledge."

"Do you know where the dragons' final resting place is located?" I asked. Ares had asked them this over a week ago, but I couldn't help but try again.

"There have been no new discoveries on that front. But the other crystal, the partner stone—we do not think that Drakon has found it yet."

Hope flared bright. "Why's that?"

"We felt a massive disturbance in the magical energy of the

world when this one was stolen from its sacred resting place. We have not yet felt that again."

"But he is close to recovering it." Ares leaned forward. "We have a contact in the League of FireSouls who was able to see into Drakon's mind. He saw that the bastard is close to finding the other stone."

"When he does find it, it will not be easy to access," the figure said. "The stone is well hidden and even better protected."

I shook my head. "It can't be protected from him. Not if he knows where it is." I pointed to the crystal on the table. "And he got that one, right?"

The figure inclined his head. "True."

"Is there anything you can tell us about where the other stone is located?" I asked.

"Yes. It is in Annatlia, near the southernmost part of Greece. Guarded by gods and legend. If you ask your dragon sense to take you there, it will. It's a mythical place, another realm located on Earth. The land of the Greek gods."

"Like Olympus?" I asked.

"Similar. Zeus rules in Olympia. But the other realms are ruled by the other Greek gods."

Hmm. That wasn't terribly descriptive.

"Do you have contacts there?" Ares asked. "Anyone that you can inform of the threat so that they can be on the alert?"

"Not us." The figure shook his head. "It is an ancient land inhabited by ancient gods. The Greeks. But you may go there and warn them yourselves."

"Not just warn them," I said. "We have to beat Drakon to it. Because whatever guards they have—they cannot stand up to him."

"And you would fare better?" the figure asked.

A wry laugh escaped me. "I'm supposed to."

~

An hour later, Ares and I arrived back in Magic's Bend. It was noon here, but the winter wind was bitter as it whipped down the street.

I pressed my fingertips to my comms charm. "Del? Cass? Meet at my place in ten, okay?"

"On it," Cass said.

"Me too," Del added.

"Later." The gleaming windows of P & P caught my eye from across the street. My stomach growled. I looked up at Ares. "Want to grab a bite on our way over?"

He nodded. We hurried into the coffee shop. The warmth and music welcomed us, as it always did. Magic sparked in the air from the enchantments in the coffee and the potions in Connor's back workshop. A couple of old men sat in the corner reading newspapers. Blue steam drifted from the tops of their coffee cups. They must be drinking a rare beverage indeed. Though Connor's enchanted coffees were imbued with magic, I hadn't seen blue steam before.

A feeling of home washed over me. As familiar and wonderful as this place was, there was always something new.

"I love this place," I murmured to Ares. It was everything good about the magical world.

And Drakon sought to take that from us. Not only would he steal our magic, and thus a part of our souls, he'd destroy everything about this place, too. It'd be wholesale slaughter down to the smallest little bit of magic. He wanted to own it all, even the enchanted blue steam.

For some reason, that made me angrier than anything.

It bubbled up in my chest, choking me. If I even started thinking about what Drakon would do once he *had* the magic....

Nope. Wasn't going to think about it.

I was going to stop him before it came to that.

"Hey, guys." Connor smiled, flipping his dark hair back from his forehead.

"Hey, Connor." I approached, noticing that he had a dustpan full of broken glass in his hand. "What's that?"

A smile tugged at the corner of his lips. "Well, you're not going to like it, but your dragon was in here."

"Jeff?"

"The very one." Connor dumped the glass in the bin behind the counter. "Seems the little guy has a taste for whiskey and thought he'd help himself."

"Oh no. He broke that, didn't he? What do I owe you?" I was going to have a talk with that little troublemaker. Talk about growing pains.

"Oddly enough, nothing." Connor picked up a gold coin from the counter and held it up. "He left me this. Recognize it?"

I took the coin. It was old and unfamiliar. "No." My mind raced. "Can Jeff make gold?"

"Why not? He's made of magic," Connor said. "And at least you don't have a thief on your hands. Clumsy, but well intentioned."

The mental image of Jeff sneaking in, fumbling the whiskey purchase, then leaving a gold coin made me smile. "I guess I'll have to ask him. But before that, could we have some pasties and coffee to go?"

"Cheese and potato for you, obviously." Connor's gaze went to Ares. "Steak and Stilton?"

"Perfect," Ares said.

Connor wrapped up the food and made the coffees, but when I tried to pay, he waved the money away. "Jeff picked up your tab."

"Uh, okay." I spoke through a laugh.

Though Drakon's dark threat loomed over us, it warmed my heart to know that there could still be moments of such unexpected joy.

I didn't know what was coming for me with Drakon. More

than likely, it'd be terrible. Deadly, even. Without a doubt the greatest challenge I would ever face.

But I had all this to fight for. My friends and family, my dragon and even the coffee shop that had become my home away from home.

I fought off the nerves and focused on my determination.

We took the coffee and pasties, thanked Connor, then headed for the door. My stomach grumbled as we stepped out into the chill winter air. Unwilling to wait, I fished the pasty out of the bag and bit into the buttery crust, enjoying the savory taste of cheese and potato.

"Don't choke," Ares said.

I swallowed and grinned at him, not surprised to see that he'd already bitten into his as well. We were so hungry that we'd polished off our lunch by the time we passed the glass storefront of Ancient Magic. My heart twinged at the sight of the closed sign and the dim interior.

Add one more thing to the pile of reasons that I needed to defeat Drakon. I needed to get back to work.

We let ourselves in through the green door and climbed the steps to my place. Del and Cass were waiting for us outside my door. Aidan and Roarke stood with them. Behind Del sat three huge dogs—hellhounds. Two black ones and a white one with brown spots. They grinned, fangs gleaming and tongues lolling.

"What are Pond Flower and her buddies doing here?" I asked.

The hellhounds were friends with Del, sensing her affinity for animals. Though they lived at the League of FireSoul's headquarters, the magical beasts had the ability to transport themselves at will. There were actually thirteen total, so I had to be grateful there were only three here.

"They showed up an hour ago, but I don't know why." Del frowned. "They haven't visited in weeks."

"Do you think they sense oncoming danger?" Ares asked. "I've heard they can do that."

"It's not the worst idea," Del said. "With Drakon, things have been getting dicey. I've been worried. Pond Flower may sense that."

Pond Flower, the white and brown dog, woofed.

"That sounds like a yes." Which made me worry even more. Magical animal were good at sensing threats.

Del turned to Pond Flower. "Can you head back home now? If there's any trouble, I'll call for you."

Pond Flower looked indecisive for a moment, then disappeared, her two friends along with her.

She was gone for now, but if trouble was brewing—which it definitely was—she'd be back.

"Did you get good news?" Cass asked me.

"I'd say so." I walked into the apartment.

Jeff snoozed on the couch, his nostrils blowing smoke.

"Sleeping it off, pal?" I asked.

His head popped up, and his gaze was alert. Looked like my little dragon could hold his liquor.

We all crowded into the small space, taking seats on the couch and leaning against the walls. Jeff got to stay on his cushion, because who the heck was going to move a dragon?

"What did you find out?" Del asked.

I told them everything we'd learned about the stone and its location. Which wasn't much.

"At least you should be able to get there," Cass said. "That's a good lead."

"Exactly. And I think we should follow it. We don't know where the dragons are yet, and we can't necessarily beat Drakon in a fight, anyway." I'd tried to kill him with a sword that could slice through anything, and it hadn't worked. I hadn't hit his heart, and that might do it, but we didn't know the size of his army. If I failed to kill them and they were there, ready to fight… No good. "So it'd be better to beat him to the battery and cut his legs out from under him."

"Without the battery stone, he can't steal the magic from the dragons," Del said. "I like it."

"Me too." I looked at them both. "I was hoping you could go to Norway to see if you can find the dragons, using your dragon sense. While you do that, Ares and I will go after the battery. We'll leave immediately."

"We can do that," Cass said.

Del nodded.

Roarke stepped forward. "I have some news from the Underworld."

I grimaced. "Oh, that's not going to be good, is it?"

Ares huffed out a wry laugh.

"No." Roarke's voice was dire. "There's word that Drakon's hired hundreds of demons to fight in a great battle. Enough demons that it could mean the apocalypse if he uses them right."

I leaned back against the couch. "Well, shit. He wants all the magic in the world *and* an apocalypse?"

"He may not want an apocalypse," Ares said. "But he does want the power to have one, should he choose."

He was all about power, that Drakon.

"How did he get the demons out of hell?" Del asked. "That's not easy."

"He didn't get them out of hell. Not most of them, at least. They're from Earth. Almost every evil demon in the world has congregated around him."

"He sent out the evil bat signal, is what you're saying," I said. Apparently his dragon tattoo gang wasn't enough. He needed more.

"Exactly."

"Do you know where these demons have gone?" Ares asked.

Roarke shook his head. "Not yet. I have scouts out looking for them. We'll find them, but it will take time."

"We don't have a lot of time," Cass said.

"Which means we need to beat Drakon to that battery." I stood, then looked at Ares. "Might as well get a move on, huh?"

CHAPTER THREE

The sun was setting when we arrived in the forest in Annatlia. It gleamed through the leaves of the oak trees, leaving dappled patterns on the ground. It'd be an idyllic wonderland if not for the tension in the air.

It prickled, swirling around the tree trunks and bombarding me. I tensed, letting go of Ares's hands and preparing to fight.

A light trill of music drifted through the forest. Like a flute almost, but reedier almost.

"You hear that?" Ares murmured.

"Yeah." I started toward it, keeping my footsteps light. "It's calling us."

Ares followed, catching up to me. The music tugged me forward, impossible to ignore. I was a fish and I was *hooked*. I wove between the trees, seeking the musician who made magic with his instrument.

I almost wasn't surprised when I came upon the man sitting in the middle of a golden ray of light cast by the setting sun. He wore no shirt and had the legs of a goat. His hooves were the same golden brown as the horns protruding from his head. A pan flute was raised to his lips.

The strong magic that I'd felt—the tension in the air—it had come from him.

He looked up at us, the music dying. His brilliant blue eyes sparked with interest.

"Pan?" I stepped closer, only a dozen feet away now.

"Who seeks me?" His voice was rough and low.

So he *was* the god Pan. "I am Phoenix Knight."

Ares stepped forward slightly. "And I am Ares Warhaven."

Pan nodded, brown curls bobbing. "I have been waiting for you, bird of flame. And Ares, gifted with our own name."

He must've been talking about Ares being named after the Greek god of war. But bird of flame? Had to be an old Greek phrase for a phoenix, right?

"Why were you expecting us?" I asked.

He arched a brow. "I *am* a god."

I winced slightly. "Right. Yeah. So you know why we're here?"

"All the gods know. We have a betting pool going. Will you defeat Drakon? Or the other way around?"

Oh man. Talk about pressure. "If the gods know that Drakon threatens all the magic in the world, why don't they do anything about it?"

Pan looked aghast. "We cannot. Nor would we. This is your fight, meant to occur on Earth, not in our realm. And the gods have heroes for a reason. You are one of those heroes, Phoenix Knight. Do not disappoint us."

Yikes. Was I really up to this? Meant to be a hero of the gods, like freakin' Hercules? Even Hercules hadn't fought to save all the magic in the world.

I couldn't help but ask, "Who are you betting on?"

"You, for what it's worth. Though after I saw that dragon…" He frowned. "I may have bet wrong."

My heart fell. "You've seen Drakon? Here?"

Pan nodded. "Yesterday. He's set off for the stone already."

Disappointment spread like black oil through my chest. "He's beaten us, then."

I didn't know where the stone was, exactly. But it wasn't nearby, and if Drakon was a day ahead of us … We were screwed.

Pan shrugged. "Possibly, though not necessarily. The stone is protected at the Temple of Athena. But there are two ways to access it. Drakon has taken the slow way."

That made no sense. "Why?"

"It was the only way open to him. The faster way is more dangerous. It requires that the person passing be worthy. He is decidedly not worthy, and the trek would have killed him."

Worthiness. There it was again. It had been the point of the trials at the Illuminarium. Now here, again. Even though fate had chosen me to defeat Drakon, I still doubted my worthiness for that. So did the world, it seemed.

"But the trek will not kill us?" Ares asked.

Pan shrugged again, a relaxed gesture that he seemed to have perfected. "I'd say you at least have a chance. And should you pass through unharmed, you may even beat Drakon to the stone. But be warned—Athena will not let anyone have it easily. She protects it from all."

We just wanted to hide the stone to protect it. Hopefully she'd understand. But first, we had to beat Drakon.

"We have to leave now," I said. "Do you have any advice for our passage? Which way to go? What we will face?"

"I cannot say what you will face, other than the gods themselves and the challenges that they have devised. Your dragon sense will lead you, but you must pass through the realms. Each territory is owned by a god and protected by them."

"So, like Hades and the Underworld, you mean?" I asked.

"Exactly. Magic will allow you to pass through the realms, where the gods may help you or harm you. Perhaps even ignore you. But be wary of my father, Hermes. He is a trickster, and the only god who can go from realm to realm."

Don't get on his bad side.

Easier said than done. The gods were finicky. And the Greek gods ... Well, they were jerks, if their myths were to be believed.

Pan held his hand out, palm up. Magic swirled around, and a mirror appeared in his palm. He handed it to me. "This is the only thing that I can give you to aid your quest. Drakon will appear in that mirror. It will gradually grow darker as he nears the stone. When lightning strikes behind him, he is there. You must beat him."

"Thank you." I looked into the mirror. The great black shadow dragon swooped through the sky, which was a pale gray behind him.

We had time. Thank fates. I tucked the mirror into my pocket.

Pan gestured to his left. "Go that way. Ask your dragon sense to take you the fastest way, regardless of danger. And don't be afraid to make tributes. They are gods. They like sacrifices."

I nodded. "Thank you."

He returned to playing his flute, a clear dismissal.

Ares and I went left, making our way through the forest. I called upon my dragon sense, asking it to take us to the Synnaroe crystal. It tugged, directing us between the trees. The air around us sparked with magic.

"We're clearly in another kind of realm," Ares said.

"Yes. But it's weird. It doesn't feel like your vampire realm." I could feel the prickly magic in the air—it was almost pleasant, rather than threatening. "It must be from the gods."

Birds twittered in the trees around us, and leaves rustled. I'd almost grown comfortable when the air in front of us shimmered darkly.

I looked at Ares. His gaze was wary as he nodded to the black mist. "We go in there?"

"Yes." I swallowed hard. "Whatever god's realm this is, I bet I'm not going to like it."

Ares reached for my hand and squeezed, then dropped it, no

doubt so that we could step through ready to fight. We approached, our footsteps light. The black mist was cold and wet against my skin.

I held my breath, then stepped through.

The chill disappeared immediately, replaced by molten heat, dry and fierce. All around, flames flickered. There was a blank space in the middle that formed a path. It was dark everywhere, save the bright orange fire.

I tensed, taking it all in. Slowly, I sucked in a shallow breath.

Though hot, the air was clean and smoke free. *Whew.* At least we could breathe.

"Only one way," Ares said.

I nodded, then stepped forward, muscles tensed. The heat grew as we neared the flames. The passage was only about ten feet wide, with walls of fire on either side.

The sound of clanging metal filled the space, as if a blacksmith were really going to town on his latest project.

"Hephaestus," I murmured. "God of fire and metal."

"And patron of the arts," Ares said. "Albeit second to Athena."

"I think we should run for it," I said. "On the count of three."

Ares nodded.

I counted down.

On three, we ran.

The heat inside the corridor was blistering—worse than Death Valley and the volcano in the Vampire realm. My lungs burned as we sprinted.

When the first whip of fire struck out, lashing for my legs, I jumped to avoid it. It struck the air below my feet. Another lick of flame struck for my head. I ducked.

Ares dodged another branch of flame.

Shit.

Quickly, I conjured a metal shield with a leather grip, then tossed it to Ares. "Take this!"

He grabbed it, using it to deflect a bolt of flame that lashed for his stomach. It collided with the shield, sending a blast of sparks. But not melting the metal, thank fates.

I conjured my own shield, using it to fend off another jet of orange fire. It slammed against the shield, harder than real fire would have. Enchanted, of course.

"Faster!" Ares yelled as he darted ahead of me.

He didn't leave me behind, just used his position to block the worst of the flames, his shield vibrating with every blow of the fire.

We sprinted, dodging and deflecting the blasts that whipped out faster and faster. Sweat poured down my face, stinging my eyes, and my heart thundered like the beat of a thousand drums.

It felt like we ran for miles.

Would this ever end?

By the time we spilled out into a clearing, my lungs felt like they were about to explode. I sucked in the cooler air, propping my hands on my knees.

"Holy fates," I panted.

"That was rough." Ares wiped at his brow, studying the space around us. "It looks like we're in a mountain."

I straightened. He was right. Though I didn't recall entering one—the black mist had only been dark, but hadn't had any structure—this was definitely a large cavern. It was the size of a football stadium, the stone dark and shiny. Overhead, thousands of sparkling red lights glinted in the rock above. They illuminated the space.

Ares pointed across the cavern. "There. An exit."

I squinted, barely able to make out the hole in the wall. A faint light glowed from it.

"That way, then." I stepped forward, muscles wobbly from the run.

We'd only gone a hundred feet—roughly to the middle of the cavern—when a massive wall of fire burst from the ground. It blocked our passage. Through the flickering flames, I could almost make out the figure of a man—huge and carrying a massive anvil.

"Hephaestus is on the other side," I said.

"I saw." Ares inspected the flames. "It's thick. There's no way through."

"I could conjure a flame retardant suit." But somehow, the idea felt wrong. I spun in a circle, studying my surroundings. "This is a game. There's a way to cross, but I don't think it's by just plowing through. Otherwise, why would Hephaestus be watching us?"

"He's a sadistic bastard who wants to watch us burn?"

"Ha. You have a point—the Greek gods were known for their ruthlessness." I tapped my chin. "But I don't think that's it."

"What about that?" Ares pointed to a circular indention in the ground.

I walked over, realizing that it was an inlaid stone circle, made of a beautiful black obsidian that flickered in the firelight. Tentatively, I touched my toe to it. Nothing happened. So I stood on it.

A vision flashed in my mind. An image of a woman, laying a small golden statue upon the obsidian slab. I gasped, stumbling back, and the vision faded. "I think we're meant to make an offering."

"That makes sense. Gods are partial to tributes."

"What would Hephaestus want, though?"

Ares frowned. "Well, he's a metalworker. A creator. Patron of the arts."

I grinned. "It's obvious, then, isn't it?"

"You want me to make him something."

I recalled the gorgeous statues in his backyard—ones that he'd created with his own hands. "Well, you are a metalsmith and an artist. And you're fast. I'd say it's almost too good to be true."

He nodded. "It's worth a try. Can you conjure me some heat resistant gloves? Leather on the inside, with fine chainmail on the outside. And several iron plates? At least two feet by four feet."

"On it." I called upon my magic, letting it flow through me, strong and true.

Thick gloves appeared in my hand. I passed them off to Ares, and he tugged them on. Then I conjured the metal plates. Three of them appeared at my feet, neatly stacked.

I stepped back, and Ares got to work. He moved so quickly I could hardly see his individual motions. He was a blur, stooping to pick up a metal plate and then thrusting it into the fire. It glowed as it heated—not molten, but certainly hot enough to become bendable.

He pulled it free and molded it with his special gloves. Sweat popped out on his skin. Though the metal was now bendable, it was clearly still a difficult task. He worked quickly, his vampire speed and strength making the job possible.

Finally, he stepped back, revealing a fabulous bird about to take flight.

"Wow." I circled the bird, eyeing its broad wings and swooping tail. It was so beautiful that my heart raced. "Is it a phoenix?"

"It is."

"Fit for a god."

A small smile tugged at the corner of Ares's mouth. A pleased smile. He went to it, picking it up as if it were made of feathers, then deposited it on the obsidian plate.

"I hope we read this right," Ares said.

"Me too." I stepped back, inspecting the wall of flame.

Suddenly, it dropped like a curtain. Hephaestus stood on the other side, anvil propped on his shoulder.

"Whoa," I whispered.

He was easily eight feet tall, with muscles stacked on top of muscles. Even human bodybuilders didn't look like he did. His face was blunt and broad, handsome in the way of bruisers and hitmen. It was impossible to mistake him as anything other than a Greek god.

This guy could snap us in half. Even Ares, though I doubted he could catch the vampire.

Hephaestus stepped forward, limping slightly. It didn't detract from his deadliness. Up close, he was even taller. His magic hit me like a sack of bricks, feeling like a burning wind and crackling flames beneath my feet.

I stiffened my stance, and it took everything I had to stay upright.

He approached the statue, his gaze riveted to the graceful lines of the phoenix as he circled the obsidian slab.

"It is impressive." His voice sounded like he spoke through a throat full of gravel.

"Thank you," Ares said.

"You have chosen a worthy offering." He swung his anvil toward the exit. "You may pass."

"Thank you." I said nothing more. Just snapped my mouth shut and walked for the exit tunnel.

Ares bowed to Hephaestus and followed.

The back of my neck tingled as we walked. We were being watched. No question.

Finally, I reached the exit, a tunnel with light gleaming at the other end. I risked one look back at Hephaestus. He had one eye on us and one on his statue. I swallowed hard and turned back, hurrying through the tunnel.

"I think that did it," I whispered.

"I think you're—"

The rock around us creaked and groaned—two sounds that rocks should never make. Then a big chunk of the ceiling fell, crashing to the ground.

"Run!" I sprinted.

Ares followed.

Rocks fell all around us. The tunnel was collapsing. I dodged boulders and leapt over debris, glancing behind me briefly to see that the tunnel was gone behind us. Rocks fell in greater numbers at our backs, closing off that direction.

I sprinted harder, lungs burning, desperate to outrace the falling stones.

Damned tricky gods.

The ground vibrated with every falling boulder, shaking my bones. Light glowed at the exit, growing larger as we neared. A beacon of hope.

We spilled out onto the forest floor as the tunnel collapsed entirely behind us. Dust billowed out, choking me.

I rolled onto my back, gasping.

"You all right?" Ares asked.

"Yeah." I conjured a bottle of water and gulped, then handed it over to him. I lay on my back, staring at the canopy overhead.

Ares drank.

"Hephaestus is a jerk." Had the god done that just for kicks?

"Agreed." He turned to me. He was flat on his back too. "You did good."

"So did you." I leaned over and kissed him. "Great phoenix."

"Great job figuring out what we needed to do." He cupped my face. "You can do this, Nix. I believe in you. I've never believed in anything so much in my life."

Tears pricked my eyes. "Thanks."

I squeezed his hand, then heaved myself up and took in our surroundings. The forest was bright, as if day had come.

"Shouldn't it be night?" I asked. "It was nearly dark when we met Pan."

"Should be, but I don't think this place is normal."

"Definitely not." I pulled the mirror from my pocket and looked at Drakon. The sky was slightly darker.

Shit.

We needed to hurry. I called on my dragon sense, letting it catch me around the middle and drag me forward.

I pointed ahead of us. "That way."

We set off through the woods, weaving between large trees.

My hair stood on end. "Feel that?"

"Like we're being watched." He looked around, his eyes alert. "But I hear no footsteps."

"Neither do I." Nor did I see anyone lurking in the trees. It was more a feeling than anything else.

Soon, we came upon a shore of a glittering blue sea. Fine white sand covered the beach. Twenty yards down, a large rock sat on the shore.

"We have to cross." I looked around for a clue. This seemed too simple. I could just conjure a boat, and we could row across. That seemed pretty easy.

Too easy.

CHAPTER FOUR

"Hey!" A voice sounded from down the beach, garbled and strange.

I turned, spotting the same rock resting on the beach. But it was moving toward us.

"A giant turtle," Ares said.

He was pale green, and at least ten feet across. I'd never seen one so big. His eyes gleamed a brilliant emerald. They stayed glued to us as he moved nearer, his flippers awkward on dry land.

"A sea turtle," I said.

"Points for the lady," the sea turtle said. "I am Nestor."

As he neared, I realized that he looked far too big for his shell. His softer bits positively burst out of the holes. Even his expression looked uncomfortable, like he was wearing a too-small shoe. Up close, the shell itself was beautiful—a shimmering green.

"What are you doing here?" Nestor demanded.

"We need to cross the sea," I said.

A crafty look entered his eyes. "Do you, now?"

"Yes. We're after the stone of Synnaroe. We need to protect it from great evil."

"Which would make this a quest!" he crowed.

33

"I suppose so, yes."

"Then you will need my help," the turtle said. "You cannot cross the sea of Poseidon in anything other than a material from the sea itself."

"Really?" Ares looked skeptically at the sea. "It looks like a regular sea."

"Hardly." Nestor shook his massive head. "But I can help you. And it won't cost you hardly a thing."

"What do you mean?" A rustling sounded from behind me. I turned and looked, but saw nothing in the forest at our backs. I turned back to the turtle.

"Well, you see, a turtle's shell can make an excellent boat. If you help me find a newer, larger shell, then I will give you my old one, and you can ride across the sea in it."

"Turtles don't change their shells. Hermit crabs, yes. Not turtles."

"You're in the land of the gods, sugar. You really think turtles follow earthly rules here?"

Sugar? Was this turtle watching TV from the 80s? "You have a point. But it's round. I've never seen a round boat. How do we steer?"

"The Welsh managed with the coracle. I'm sure you can as well."

True enough. The ancient round boat of the early Welsh had been effective.

"But it has holes in it," I said.

"Bah! Cover them with something." Nestor shook his head. His gaze was still crafty, but his mouth turned down at the edges. A turtle frown. "It will be a good deal for you. And a good deed."

"How so?"

"I am desperate. Not only am I uncomfortable and it is too difficult for me to travel on land to retrieve my own new shell, I am trying to pursue my dream. And you can help me."

"What dream?" Ares asked.

The turtle hesitated just briefly. Either he was too shy to share his dream or he was coming up with one.

Nah. I shouldn't doubt him right off the bat.

Nestor sucked in a breath. "I want to be a member of Poseidon's fleet of carriage-pulling sea turtles. I've waited all my life to grow big enough—which is really quite a while, if you must know—but now I need a bigger shell. It's a matching fleet, so I must match."

"That's quite a story," Ares said.

Nestor glared. "It's not a story! It's my dream."

I'd give the turtle credit—he really sold the tale. If it weren't so ridiculous, I could almost imagine Poseidon riding in a carriage pulled by a dozen matching sea turtles. But his eyes looked crafty. This turtle was taking us for a ride.

A rustling sounded from behind me again. I turned, catching sight of a flash of gold just before it disappeared.

"Well?" Nestor prodded. "Will you help me? I can tell you exactly where the shell is. It will only take you five minutes."

"Why can't you do it, then?"

"My shell is too big to fit between the forest trees, and the shell is on top of a rock. I cannot reach it."

"Hmm. Let me confer with my friend," I said.

The turtle nodded.

I gestured to Ares, and we moved a dozen feet away. I leaned in and whispered, "This smells fishy."

"Yes. Poseidon is known for his horses and carriage, not turtles."

I nodded, then caught sight of another flash of gold in the forest, low, near the ground. For a second, it looked like a little wing.

Winged shoes.

"I think Hermes is here," I whispered. "In the forest."

"Trickster god."

"Yeah." I racked my brain, trying to think of *why* the turtle would want this. Though it could be devious, sometimes the truth really was the most obvious thing. "I think we should help him. He's clearly miserable."

"We don't have a lot of time."

"No, I know. You're right. But it's only five minutes. And he looks so unhappy. We can't leave him like this. With your speed, it might be even quicker." I frowned. "And remember. We're in the world of myth now. Quests like these shouldn't be ignored."

Ares nodded. "Valid point. But if it's more than a five-minute task, it's too much of a risk."

"Fair." I turned back to the turtle and approached. "We will help you, but be honest … If it is going to take more than five minutes, we will have to return and help you after we save the stone of Synnaroe. But I vow that we will return."

"Only five minutes, I promise," Nestor said. "And you need my shell anyway, as it is the only way to cross the sea. So you must help me."

"I can conjure us a boat," I reminded the turtle. "I'm a conjurer."

"Won't do you much good when Poseidon claims it for his own."

I frowned, not wanting to believe him. But there was every chance he was right. "Fine. Tell us where to find your shell."

"Not far." He gestured with a big flipper, back into the woods. "That way, not a two-minute run away from the sea, sitting on top of some rocks."

I nodded and looked at Ares. "Ready for a quest?"

"Always."

"Then this time, use your speed. I'll try to keep up."

He nodded and we hurried off, back through the woods. Ares raced ahead, disappearing into the forest.

I caught up with him two minutes later, just in time to see him standing on top of a massive pile of rocks, the huge shell balanced on his head like a coin on its edge.

He jumped down. I panted, admiring him. Frankly, it was a ridiculous feat of physical prowess.

I gazed up at the shell, which rose fifteen feet above his head. "Think you can run like that?"

"Yes."

"All right, then. Let's go." I turned and raced back through the forest, Ares sprinting ahead of me.

When I arrived back on the beach, the new shell was already laid in front of Nestor. We'd completed the task in four minutes, max.

Not bad.

He had a big turtle grin on his face as he wiggled inside of his old shell, yanking his fat flippers back in through the holes, then shimmying out of the hole where his head protruded. Magic swirled around him as he scurried across the sand to his new shell. His green form looked a bit squishy and strange—no wonder he needed a shell.

As he was making himself comfortable inside his new home, I approached the old shell that he'd promised to give us.

Before I reached it, a golden blur shot from the trees and jumped on top of the shell.

The man grinned at us.

Hermes.

No question about it. He looked like a California beach dude, with gleaming curls and a tan. Golden winged shoes fluttered at his feet. His magic pulsed on the air, feeling like a brisk wind and tasting of water.

"That's our shell," I said.

"Not anymore." He grinned.

I looked at Nestor in time to see the crafty gleam in his eyes. "You tricked us, turtle."

Nestor sighed. "It's all part of the test, of course."

I glared at him, then Hermes, who also looked pretty tricky.

"What test? If you wanted the shell, Hermes, couldn't you just have helped Nestor yourself?"

"I was prohibited from climbing the pile of rocks upon which it sat. So Nestor and I came up with this plan."

Ares frowned and crossed his arms over his chest, but said nothing. Clearly he didn't approve of the trickery.

"Whatever," I muttered. "Keep your shell. I'll conjure us a boat."

"Do not waste the magic," Hermes said. "Poseidon will claim any craft that does not come from his own sea."

"Then we do need that shell," Ares said.

I glanced quickly at him, noting the warrior's stance. *Please don't try to fight a god.*

I didn't want to play Hermes's games, nor did I want a fight. So I conjured a small model of a boat, then set it down at the edge of the sea. The little boat floated on the crystal blue water, and I gave it a good push, letting it glide farther out. It floated on the sparkling surface, drifting deeper and deeper.

Then sank like a stone.

Hermes grinned. "You see?"

He was clearly loving this. Jerk.

"What do you want for the shell?" I asked.

He tapped his chin. "Hmmm."

"Wait," Nestor said. "Do not deal with him. He may ask the impossible."

"Then what do we do?" Ares asked.

"I will carry you over on my back." Nestor nodded. "You helped me, and I will repay that."

Hermes scowled, but Nestor shot him a "what are you going to do about it?" look.

"Deal." Maybe I should have thought about it longer—considered all the options, since he could technically drop us in the middle of the sea—but we were desperate. And Hermes did look tricky. After the move Hephaestus had pulled on us, I didn't want to deal with another god if I could help it.

Ares met my gaze, a question in his own.

"We should try to have faith," I murmured.

"I won't let you down," Nestor said.

"I hope not."

Hermes looked disappointed, but I ignored him. He'd gotten what he wanted.

Nestor dragged himself into the shallows, his green shell shimmering against the glittering blue sea. Ares and I climbed onto his back. It was pleasantly rough, providing me with enough grip so that I didn't slip off. I perched on the top, Ares at my side.

Joy bubbled up inside me. I was riding a giant sea turtle!

"Oof," Nestor said. "You really need to lay off the Twinkies."

"Twinkies?" I laughed.

"They're my favorite human food. Aren't they yours?"

"No. But if you get us across safely, I'll conjure you some Twinkies."

Nestor turned his massive head to look back at us, his eyes sparkling. "Really?"

"Really."

He nodded. "A deal, then."

I felt a bit better, knowing that he wanted those Twinkies on the other end. He'd probably be more likely to deliver us.

Nestor pushed off into the sea. Water lapped at the edges of our living raft, but we were high enough that we'd stay dry as long as there were no big waves.

I turned to watch the receding shore. Hermes was staring after us, brow creased. I couldn't make out the expression in his eyes, which made unease prickle at the back of my neck.

I did not want to be on a god's bad side.

"Think he's pissed at us?" I asked Ares.

"Hard to say," Ares said.

"Eh, Hermes is all right," Nestor said. "Though your buddy is right. He's a tough one to read. He could still pull a nasty trick on you, so just hope you don't see him again."

It was all we could do. I snuck a peak at the mirror in my pocket. Drakon was flying but it was not yet dark, thank fates.

The ride across the sea was beautiful. It sparkled like blue diamonds the whole way across, the sun hanging high overhead. Nestor kept up a steady pace. I couldn't help but peer into the water, hoping for a glimpse of Poseidon. Or worse, a kraken.

But when the threat came, it dove from above.

I heard the rush of wings and glanced up, just in time to see a massive albatross with serrated teeth diving straight for us.

"Bird!" I screamed.

"Hold tight!" Nestor yelled.

I gripped at a ridge in his shell, heart thundering. I sucked in a deep breath and Nestor dove. Water engulfed me. I hung on for dear life as water rushed around me. Though the salt water stung my eyes, I kept them open.

Ares held on next to me. It was bright blue beneath the sea. Nestor was so fast that I couldn't maintain my sitting position. Instead, I dangled off his back as we shot through the water.

My lungs burned as we raced along beneath the sea. All around us, the albatross shot into the water like torpedoes, brilliant white bubbles exploding around them. There were dozens of the large birds.

Below, I caught a brief glimpse of a fabulous castle beneath the sea. Poseidon's lair. Excitement thrilled through me.

I wanted to scream at Nestor to go up for air. My muscles were weakening without oxygen, my grip slackening.

As if he sensed my problem, Ares grabbed me around the waist, holding me tight to him. By the time Nestor burst to the surface, black dots were dancing in front of my vision. I sucked in air, gasping and choking. The dots faded.

I glanced back, frantic to see if the albatross were coming for us. Instead, they floated on the surface far behind us, wet and bedraggled.

I gasped. "Why aren't they chasing?"

"Not great divers, those carnivorous albatross," Nestor said. "It'll take them a while to dry off enough to fly again."

"Then why did they dive?" Ares asked.

"They get excited. Can't help themselves." Nestor laughed. "Dumb birds."

I sucked in air as I struggled to a sitting position. Next to me, Ares appeared to be fine.

"Why aren't you out of breath?" I asked.

"Giant lungs. All that running," he said.

So it wasn't just magic that made him fast, but also strength and practice.

"Well, thanks for keeping me on. It was getting dicey there for a while." I kept my gaze wary the rest of the way, eyes peeled for any more albatross or other threats. By the time the shore appeared on the horizon, I was more than ready for my turtle ride to be over.

As we neared, dread began to chill my skin. We weren't approaching the lovely forest and white sand beach of the land we'd left behind. No—this was far darker, with twisted white trees and a black sand beach. Even the sky was darker, as if it were perpetually night over the forest.

"What is this place?" I asked.

"Hades's realm," Nestor said. "I will not stay long. You must be quick."

"I thought it was underground," Ares said.

"A modern human interpretation," Nestor said. "It is accessed by the sea. Or the rivers Acheron or Styx, from the other side."

"Shit." My gaze traveled over it. Though rationally I knew that all of the gods were pretty jerky and any of their realms might hold death for us, this was freaking Hades.

Hell.

The water lost its sparkling blue shine as we neared, turning gray and murky. It lapped at the edges of Nestor's shell, leaving a brown stain.

"Quickly now," Nestor said as he beached on the shore. "And don't forget my Twinkies."

I scrambled off, Ares behind me, then turned. Quickly, I conjured four Twinkies. One by one, I tossed them into Nestor's mouth. His eyes gleamed as he chomped merrily.

I tossed the last one. "Thank you, Nestor."

Nestor smacked his lips. "Thank you." He shuffled back into the water and swam back to sea as quickly as he could.

The back of my neck tingled, and I turned to face the forest. It was about twenty yards away, across the black beach. The trees were an eerie ivory color and the leaves black as pitch. Though there were similarities to some of the vampire realm forests, it was different. Worse.

"Does it feel like it has eyes?"

"Yes." Ares studied the forest, his muscles tensed.

I swallowed hard and started toward the forest, skin prickling with wariness. As we neared, the ivory trees shifted.

I stopped dead in my tracks. "Oh, fates. Are those bones?"

"Yes."

Every tree was made of bones, pale and white. Thousands of them. And the black leaves were actually … bats. They perched on all the branches, thousands of them.

I sucked in a ragged breath and continued forward. As we neared, a sickness welled inside me. Queasiness spread up from my stomach, filling my whole chest.

"Do you feel that?" I asked.

"No, what's wrong?"

"My magic feels weaker. Like it's repressed."

"Your life magic won't interact with the death magic here, possibly."

"Yeah, I think you're right." I pushed myself forward, heart thundering. I did *not* like the idea of going in there with weakened magic.

We were nearly to the trees when the first one lashed out, a limb made of hundreds of bones snapping toward us. Bats took off into the sky.

I dove out of the way, rolling in the black sand.

I scrambled to my feet. "Shit! Does *everything* in this world like to whip out at you?"

"Apparently so."

I conjured two shields, grateful that this magic was working, at least. "Hades needs to get some new plans. Hephaestus already did that."

Ares gave me a sharp look. "Don't piss off the gods."

I winced. "Yeah, good point." I turned to the forest. "I like your trees, Hades. Very threatening."

Ares chuckled. "I'm sure he didn't see through that *at all*."

"I'll just keep my mouth shut." It was one thing to say something stupid at a party. Entirely another to do so in front of the vindictive Greek gods.

We edged closer to the forest, waiting for the tree's attack. They stilled as we entered.

Immediately, hunger struck me. Hard.

"You feel that?" Ares asked.

"Yes. I'm starving."

"Magic."

I nodded, trying to ignore the hunger. Though part of me wanted to conjure a banana or something, I didn't want to let my guard down long enough to eat. And since this was magic induced, I doubted it would help.

"Let's keep going." I crept through the forest, my shield held high.

The bats sitting in the trees of bones watched us pass. Deeper into the forest, bright red fruits appeared on the limbs. My stomach grumbled. Desperately, I wanted to reach for one.

"Pomegranates," Ares said.

"Shit." I licked my lips. "Isn't that what Persephone ate? Then she had to stay in the underworld part of the year."

"Yes. Don't eat of the fruits of hell."

"Got it." I stared resolutely forward, ignoring the shiny red fruits.

Something shimmered on the air, feeling distinctly like irritation. Like the forest was growing weary of our resistance. The trees trembled, as if desperate to strike out. A pomegranate shot off the tree. I threw up my shield to block the fruit. Then more came, shooting towards us.

I tried blocking them all, but there were too many. One nailed me in the thigh, a hard blow that would leave a hell of a bruise. "Ouch!"

"Run," Ares said.

We sprinted through the forest, darting between the trees. The fruits flew left and right. I could block the ones that went for my body, but my legs were unprotected. Every time one of the heavy, hard-shelled fruits nailed me, I stumbled.

Then, the bats came. They shrieked as they launched themselves from the trees, dive-bombing us. I shielded my face with an arm, sprinting full out. The little beasts collided with my body, sinking their teeth in deep. Occasionally they'd pierce the fabric of my jeans or get a bite into my bare hand.

Soon, my lungs were burning and all of me hurt like hell. I called on my dragon sense, begging it to find us a cave or something to hide in.

"We need to find cover!" Ares yelled.

"You read my thoughts!" I yelled.

I'd just latched onto a location when a voice boomed through the forest. "Stop!"

I halted in my tracks, skidding on the ground. Ares, as if compelled, did the same.

I lowered my arm, panting, and peeked out. The bats and

pomegranates had frozen in midair. A beautiful woman stood in front of me. She wore a Greek-style dress and had golden threads of wheat woven through her hair. Her magic was a balm to my soul, flowing out of her like a rush of cool water and the feel of rich, life-giving dirt. She held a torch that glowed bright, making her look like she stood in a pool of sunlight.

I dropped my arm. "Persephone!"

A cocky smile tugged at her lips. "How did you know?"

"Your magic. And the wheat in your hair."

"Well done. And you are Phoenix Knight, our newest hero."

"I sure hope so."

"You doubt yourself?" she asked.

I shrugged. "Maybe."

"You shouldn't." She looked at Ares. "He doesn't. Ares Warhaven believes in you. Should I?"

"That's a doozy of a question." I glanced warily at the bats, grateful to see that they were still frozen in midair.

"Then why don't you answer one for me?"

"Okay."

"You will have a choice of two monsters to fight when you attempt to reach the River Acheron to leave this place. Would you rather fight the Empusa or Medusa?"

"I know who Medusa is. But what is the Empusa?"

"The Empusa is the daughter of Hecate and the spirit Mormo. She was born evil, her only desire to devour the flesh and blood of others. She has hair of flame, dagger teeth, and the wings of a bat. Though there is a small chance you can defeat her, your chances are much better against Medusa. You must only avoid looking into her eyes so that you aren't turned to stone. But if you want to escape her, you must kill her. It would not be terribly difficult, as she is not much of a fighter."

I scoffed. "That's easy. I'll take the Empusa."

Ares glanced sharply at me, as if surprised that I would choose the more dangerous monster.

Persephone's brows rose. "And why is that?"

"Medusa isn't really a monster, according to Ovid. She was cursed because Poseidon raped her in Athena's temple. Athena was so angry that she turned Medusa into the monster she is today. So I'm not going to sign up to kill her."

Persephone nodded. "You know your history."

"And the difference between right and wrong."

"That as well." She waved me forward. "Come with me. I will help you."

"Will Hades be okay with that?" I asked.

"Ha! Hades. He thinks he owns me. But I do as I please during my time here. And I will help you. Your magic is that of life, like mine. And you've chosen wisely twice. You've helped my friend Nestor, and you chose to fight the correct monster. You are worthy, Phoenix Knight."

I liked hearing it, but really, I'd just done what anyone would do. I didn't see how it made me worthy if everyone would do it.

But I didn't argue, just followed along behind her.

"Move quickly, now," Persephone said. "My magic will not hold them forever."

We ran through the forest, following her between the trees of bones. They didn't attack us as long as we were with Persephone. Finally, the trees thinned as we neared a cave.

Persephone ducked inside. "Come."

Her torch lit the gray stone walls of the cave. It was narrow and tight. My breath drew short. I *hated* tiny places like this.

We squeezed through, going deeper and deeper into the mountain, until finally, we reached a room of medium size that had an enormously tall ceiling. A beam of light filtered down from the ceiling, shining upon a silver helmet that sat upon a pedestal in the middle of the room.

I gasped. "Is that Hades's helmet of invisibility?"

Persephone grinned. "It is. He has no idea that I have it. I requested that Hephaestus make me a replica, and I left it in his armory. Now, whenever he puts it on, I pretend that I can't see him."

"He buys that?"

"A guy with an ego as big as his? Sure. He never saw it coming."

"Why did you do it?" Ares asked.

She shrugged. "Why not? Sometimes I like to be invisible. And this place is protected from him. The light conceals it from his gaze."

"Well done." My gaze all but stroked the gleaming silver. What an incredible artifact.

"You may wear it to escape here. It will help you get past the Empusa. If you hold Ares's hand, he, too, will be invisible. When you get to the river Acheron, leave it with the child of Cerberus."

"A miniature three-headed dog?"

"Two-headed." She smiled. "His third has yet to come in."

Like baby teeth. But heads. "Okay. Thank you."

She nodded. "You must hurry. Beat Drakon to the stone of Synnaroe. You are the world's only hope, Phoenix."

I swallowed hard and nodded, determined to be worthy. "Thank you. Truly."

I reached for the helmet and put it on. The metal was heavy and smooth. Cold magic chilled me, dripping down my skin like water. The invisibility charm. I gripped Ares's hand, and he shivered as the magic washed over him.

"It works." Persephone grinned, then pointed to a passage on the other side of the room. "Follow that next passage there. It will lead you to the Empusa's territory. Try not to let her hear you. Get past her, then cross the river Acheron. Do not forget to give the helmet to the child of Cerberus."

"I won't. Thank again." I then turned and ran for the tunnel. Ares gripped my hand tightly, jogging alongside. Fortunately, this tunnel was wider. But the way was long. By the time we spilled out into the dark forest on the other side, I was grateful to be in open air.

We stilled to take in our surroundings. The trees here were made of bones, but the bats were gone, leaving the branches bare. The ground was barren and rocky. Silence reigned.

I nodded at Ares, and we set off, running through the forest as quietly as we could. My dragon sense pulled us along, directing us toward the River Acheron. Our exit.

The first flap of wings made my hair stand on end. Though I wanted to look back, I pushed myself forward, desperately trying to control my breathing.

The shriek nearly made me stumble. All around, thousands of bats fluttered alongside. Ah, hell. Empusa's minions?

CHAPTER FIVE

Overhead, heat blazed. The flap of wings was so loud. I chanced a glance upward, catching sight of flaming hair and fangs so long they could pierce straight through my neck.

Ice raced through my veins.

The Empusa swept past us, her leathery black wings carrying her through the air.

She hadn't seen us.

But she swooped back, flying low over the trees, her blazing red eyes searching the ground below. Her hands were tipped with white talons that could shred the flesh from my bones.

I ran harder, gripping Ares's hand. If I let go and she saw him....

The bats coalesced around us, as if they could sense us more easily than the Empusa. Their little wings brushed against my arms and face. Shivers raced over me.

The Empusa swooped down at us, drawn by the bats.

I dove low, dragging Ares with me. We skidded on the ground, narrowly avoiding the Empusa's raking claws, then scrambled upright.

My muscles were burning as we ran, the bats and the Empusa so close that the flap of their wings was the only thing I could hear.

When the trees began to thin and the Empusa shrieked her rage, hope gave me an extra shot of energy. We hurtled from the forest, skidding to a stop at a river bank.

I clutched Ares's hand tight and spun. The Empusa hovered in midair at the tree line, her gaze searching the shore of the river.

"She can sense us," Ares whispered.

"But she can't approach."

Her minions flew around her. She vibrated with rage, her black dress trembling. Her hair blazed out from her head, a fiery orange that somehow complimented her massive fangs.

"Do you think she barbecues people with her hair before she eats them?" I whispered.

Ares choked back a laugh. The Empusa's head shifted towards us, her gaze narrowing. Chills raced over my spine.

Barking sounded from our left. I turned. A two-headed dog the size of a horse galloped along the riverbank, his fiery red eyes trained on the Empusa. He charged right up to the forest, growling and snapping.

The Empusa hissed and wheeled away, disappearing back through the forest. Her bats followed.

The hound turned to face us, its two heads nearly identical save for the different colored eyes. One had red eyes, the other orange. His fur was a shiny black. Muscles rippled underneath.

"*He's* a puppy?" I said.

"I'd hate to see his father."

The child of Cerberus trotted toward us. Though menace rolled off of him, I barely felt worried at all. I slipped off the helmet and handed it out to him, then let go of Ares's hand.

He woofed low, then took the helmet in his jaws. Well, one of his jaws. The one with orange eyes. The other head reached out and licked my hand.

"Ouch!" I shook my hand. His tongue was as rough as sandpaper. It'd left little red scrapes. I shook a finger at him. "You're very sweet, but you have to be careful."

He woofed low.

Ares chuckled. "You're scolding a hound of hell?"

"Please. Del has a hellhound. You met Pond Flower. They're just dogs." I bent down and picked up a stick, then tossed it. The dog jumped, spinning in midair, then took off after the stick. I dusted my hands together. "See?"

Ares grinned. "Point taken. Ready to cross this river?"

"As I'll ever be." I turned back to it.

The water was an oily black, like thousands of gallons of ink. Oddly, it smelled like metal. About thirty yards away, a boatman punted across the river. He wore a long black cloak that concealed his whole form, making him look like the grim reaper.

"Want to try for a ride?" I asked.

"Sure."

We jogged down the beach, reaching the ferryman just as he beached his small boat on the shore.

"Hi." I stepped forward. "Can we get a ride?"

His head tilted up. Though he had no features—just a gaping black space where a face should have been—his eyes gleamed red. His magic felt like flames licking against my skin.

"This isn't the River Styx. And I'm not for sale." His voice held all the rough darkness of hell, and I shivered.

"Um. I'm sorry." I held up my hands, placating. "No offense meant. Perhaps you could just help us? Please?"

"No." His voice whipped out, ice cold. "This task is for you, not me. You shall not find the underworld so accommodating."

He lifted his pole and pushed off of the bank, sending his boat drifting back across the river.

I turned to Ares. "Well, shit."

"Could you try conjuring?"

"Yes." Though I'd hoped to save the power, especially since

hell suppressed a lot of my magic, this was necessary. I called upon my gift, envisioning a small wooden rowboat. It appeared on the shore, half of it floating in the shallows of the river. Last, I conjured two oars. I turned to Ares. "Ready?"

He nodded. I climbed on first, moving toward the stern. Ares jumped in then pushed off the bank. As soon as the boat was floating freely in the water, it began to sink.

"But there are no holes!" I cried. My boat was perfect.

But the inky water devoured it. Soon, it lapped at the tops of my boots, burning my skin. Then at my knees and thighs. Agony swept through me, then despair. Sadness like I'd never known clawed at my mind.

"Back to the shore!" Ares's voice was pained.

"No!" It was up to my chest now. "We have to swim for it. Quickly!"

There was no other way. With my perfect boat sinking and the only native hell-made boat now out of sight, swimming was our only shot.

"Hurry, then," Ares gritted.

The water was up to my neck, bringing with it pain and sadness. My skin felt like it was burning, and horrible thoughts and memories bombarded my mind. It was as if the water were made of Phantoms. But this was just the nature of the River Acheron. Each of the rivers in hell had a characteristic. Unfortunately, we had to swim through the worst one.

I struck out through the black water, kicking as hard as I could. When my arms broke the surface, they were coated with inky black water.

Tears rolled down my cheeks as I swam, thoughts of failure filling my mind. What if I couldn't beat Drakon? What if everyone in the world lost their magic because of me?

What would we lose? Not just our magic, but our way of life. Drakon would use his ill-gotten gains to subjugate the world.

Nothing was past him. He could turn us all into prisoners. Or slaves. Or kill us all. He was so evil that his end goal could be anything—but no matter what, it would be the annihilation of everything I knew and loved.

What would happen to my *deirfiúr* ? To Ares?

I swam through the pain, turning my misery into determination.

At the middle of the river, the water turned thicker. Almost like pudding. Ares swam next to me, even his strong strokes faltering.

A cold laugh sounded from the bank behind us. I managed to turn my head just enough to catch a glimpse of a huge man. He wore ancient armor, and his eyes were black as coal.

Hades.

"I'm doing this for all of us, you know," I shouted back at him, suddenly angry. I didn't expect help from all the gods, but his cold laughter in the face of my pain? *Bastard.*

I kicked harder, rage propelling me in a way that grief couldn't. I pushed myself, dragging my body through the mucky water. By the time we reached the other shore, my muscles were trembling and achy, my face soaked with tears.

I crawled out of the muck, thoroughly coated. Hades's cold laughter died. I flopped onto my back, panting, and turned my head.

He was gone. I could almost feel the annoyance he'd left on the air. "Take that, jerk."

Ares struggled upright, then reached a hand down for me. "Come on, there's a clear pool up ahead. We have to wash this stuff off."

He was right. It still burned, and the grief brought by the river still lurked at the corners of my mind. I dragged myself up and followed him to the clear pool, taking in the forest around us.

It was lovely, actually, a mass of silver birches. The sun shined dimly through the trees, as if it were dawn. Birds chirped. The water in the small pond glittered crystal clear, the pebbles at the bottom a bright, shiny silver.

I stumbled into the water alongside Ares. It was cool and fresh, washing away the black ink. The pain faded, and the grief drifted from my mind. I sagged, submerging my head and letting the water wash away my tears.

With the misery gone, all that was left was the memory of what I was fighting for. Strength filled me. Inspiration. I could not fail at this—even if I didn't think I was worthy, I *had* to be.

Lungs burning, I pushed myself to the surface. Ares had just broken through as well. His hair was slicked back from his head and his face clean of the black inky water.

His gaze zeroed in on mine immediately.

My heart thumped, swelling with an unfamiliar emotion that felt a hell of a lot like—

"I love you." He dragged me against him, clutching me close. His voice was raspy at my ear. "In the river, I faced my greatest fear. Losing you. And it became clear … I love you."

Lightness and joy filled my chest. *Yes. Yes.* This was right. It was so right. The River of Acheron had stripped away all of the unnecessary bullshit that clouded my mind and taken me down to pure fear and loss.

And one of the things I'd feared losing most was Ares. Like my *deirfiúr* .

And he felt the same.

My heart felt like it would burst out of my chest as I pulled back and met his gaze. Love burned in the depths of his green eyes, so obvious. I'd always thought it sounded trite when I read it in books, but I was *so damned wrong.*

I pressed my lips to his, kissing him hard. "I love you, too." I laughed, a slightly crazed sound. "Holy shit, I do."

I blinked, suddenly full of strength and determination. I had so much to fight for. I always had, and even if I hadn't, I'd have fought anyway. The fight was that important.

But now, with Ares….

"I want more of this." The words spilled out of me. "A lifetime of it."

"So do I." He kissed me hard. "Which means we need to get started. We have to get to that stone before Drakon does."

"Yes." I pulled back and swam for the shore to climb out.

Ares joined me, shaking his limbs as water flew off. My clothes dripped, heavy and wet.

I pulled the mirror from my pocket, grateful to see it uncracked. Within, Drakon flew. Behind him, the sky was a dark gray.

Shit. Almost out of time. My heart thumped.

I was about to conjure a fresh set of clothes when a voice sounded from behind me.

"Well, I cannot say that I am not impressed."

I turned. Hermes stood at the other side of the pond, his golden sandals glinting in the dim sunlight.

"How long have you been there for?" I didn't like the idea of him witnessing the moment between me and Ares.

"Just a moment. Long enough to see you crawl out of this pond like a primordial creature."

Whew.

"You may be impressed, but Hades wasn't," I said.

"Miserable bastard, Hades," Hermes said. "But can you blame him?"

"I guess not," I said. "What did you do with Nestor's shell?"

"Added it to my collection." He grinned. "You would know all about that."

I thought longingly of my trove. "I would, though turtle shells aren't my thing."

"You don't know what you're missing." Hermes's voice was rapturous.

Okay, Hermes was a nut job, apparently.

"I am here because I was impressed," Hermes said. "You passed my test—with Nestor—and then you passed Persephone's. Well done, the two of you. Thus I am here to give you a tip. A hint."

"What kind?" Ares asked.

"You have entered the realm of Artemis, goddess of forests and the hunt. It will not be easy to pass through, but if you hope to make it out alive, I suggest you find her temple and make an offering."

"A sacrifice?" Ares asked.

"Yes."

"But not a dead animal or anything?" I shuddered.

"No. Artemis frowns on others killing the animals in her realm. She is the only huntress here."

"Okay, then something of value," I said.

"Exactly. And I have one more thing to assist you. Something that I gave to the hero who came before you."

"Perseus?" Ares asked.

"Indeed." Hermes held out his hand, and two pairs of golden, winged sandals dangled from his grip.

My heart leapt. *No freaking way.*

So far, being the chosen one had mostly come with a lot of danger and fear. But this? This was really cool.

"Thank you." My voice was breathless.

"Thank me after you have learned to use them," he said. "Because you'll need to be skilled to escape Artemis on her hunt."

"Oh, shit." My skin chilled. "So, we're looking at the deadliest game, huh?"

Hermes shrugged. "Artemis doesn't normally make a habit of hunting people, but she doesn't like trespassers. You must make it to her temple and leave an appropriate offering in order to avoid her wrath."

But first we have to make it to her temple.

I took the sandals from Hermes and handed off a pair to Ares. Before we could strap them on, Hermes stepped forward and waved a hand toward us. A blast of warm, dry air rushed over me, drying my clothes instantly.

"Thanks." I smiled.

Hermes nodded.

We put on our sandals over the tops of our boots. As soon as I'd tied the last lace, I shot straight into the air. My head bumped on a tree limb. Pain shot through me.

"Ow!"

"Careful!" Hermes called. "Envision where you want to go. Send your will to the sandals."

I imagined fluttering lightly to the ground. I dropped suddenly, struggling to slow my descent right before I crashed. Next to me, Ares hovered effortlessly above the ground. I glared at him.

He shrugged. "Vampire reflexes."

"I'm trying again." This time, I wobbled slowly upward, but managed to keep from nailing the branch again.

Victory.

Hermes winced, clearly not agreeing. "Because I'd like to ensure that you complete your mission against Drakon, I will lead you to the temple of Artemis. At least that way, you can focus on your flying instead of your dragon sense."

"Thank you!" I would take it. A guide was not to be turned down. No way.

"Just follow me, then, and avoid the arrows."

Arrows? *Shoot.*

Ha. Bad pun.

Hermes launched himself into the air, gracefully ascending above the trees. I wobbled my way up to him, grateful to have Ares at my side. By the time I crested the tops of the birches, I had the hang of it. A bit. At least, I was no longer wobbling.

Hermes darted off across the treetops. I imagined following him, and my sandals complied. I zipped across the air after him.

Joy filled me as we flew toward a large white temple on a hill. It looked like the Parthenon, though we were definitely not in Athens.

By the time the sound of thudding hoofbeats sounded below, I was floating on cloud nine.

"Incoming!" Hermes shouted.

I startled, looking down. A glorious woman rode a massive steed, cantering between the trees, her bow pointed upward. Golden hair flew behind her head. An arrow flew fast and true—straight for me.

Shit!

I dodged left, barely missing the arrow and scraping against some tree branches that clawed at my hair. I righted myself, darting after Hermes and Ares. The next arrow sailed for Ares, but he nimbly dodged it.

"That's the way!" Hermes did an excited loop-de-loop.

I struggled to keep my balance, my gaze constantly darting to Artemis on her horse. Her bow was an incredible work of art, a masterpiece.

One that was shooting straight at me.

I dodged left, hearing the arrow whistle past my ear. Sweat broke out on my skin, chilling in the breeze. I darted after the golden Hermes. The temple was only fifty yards away, now. The massive white columns gleamed in the sun.

Ares dodged another arrow, lunging high into the air. The next one came for me. Though I darted, scraping the tops of the trees, the arrowhead sliced through my arm. Pain blazed.

I ignored it, grateful that the arrow shaft wasn't embedded in my flesh, and hurtled through the columns of the temple. I dove for the ground and rolled to a stop on the marble floor.

Hermes stood calmly after a perfect descent. So did Ares. I

scrambled to my feet in the open space. The roof soared high above, but there were no walls between the massive columns that supported it.

"We're here to make a tribute!" I called.

Hermes winced. "Not necessary to say it out loud. It is quite obvious from the fact that you are here."

"Oh, okay." I nodded awkwardly. "Just wanted to make sure we didn't get shot again."

"Again?" Ares's sharp gaze darted over me.

I held out my arm. The arrow had sliced so cleanly through my jacket sleeve that the wound wasn't visible underneath the leather, but it stung like the devil. "Just a flesh wound. Let's worry about it after the tribute."

He frowned, clearly not liking the plan, then nodded.

Good. Glad he was on board. Getting shot again was definitely a bigger threat.

I studied the open, empty space of the temple, noting the large altar on the other side. I approached it, Ares at my side. We stopped in front of it, staring at the empty space.

"Too bad there are no other tributes," I said. "It'd be nice to have a hint."

"Something that is valuable to you," Hermes said. "That's what the gods like best. Then it's a true sacrifice."

"Hmm, all right." I racked my brain. "I don't have anything of value on me right now. And if I conjure it, then it can't be that special, can it?"

Ares shook his head. "That won't work. But I do have my shadow sword."

He drew it from the ether. The blade flickered with black flame.

Hermes whistled low. "That *is* impressive."

"No!" I touched Ares's arm. "You made the offering to the Hephaestus. I should do this one. Anyway, it's my challenge."

And he'd never be able to replace that sword. I couldn't let him give it up.

"What if I offer to help Artemis find anything she wants—anything in the world?" I hesitated. "As soon as we've defeated Drakon, that is. It'd be a risk for me if she wanted something dangerous. Perhaps even deadly."

"Hmmm." Hermes tapped his chin.

The clip clop of horse hooves sounded, then a feminine voice. "Oh, quit trying to look thoughtful, Hermes."

Hermes scowled, then disappeared into thin air.

I turned. Artemis rode her horse into the temple, tall and strong.

Whoa. Bad-ass.

"Would that work?" I asked. "I rarely help anyone find anything. It's a carefully guarded skill. But I'll do it for you, as my tribute."

A thoughtful gleam entered Artemis's eye. "Yes, that will do."

She dismounted in a graceful leap, then strode toward me. Her leather armor was studded with iron. Very cool. She flicked her wrist, and a piece of parchment appeared in her hand. Then a quill.

She stopped in front of me, silver eyes assessing. Then she nodded and handed over the quill and parchment. "Your blood will act as ink."

"Uh, sure!" Ugh, gods.

"Just press the tip to your wrist."

Oh, man. This was dumb, wasn't it? Making a blood vow to the gods. I steeled myself—this *was* necessary—and pressed the tip of the quill to my wrist. Pain flared and blood welled. The quill soaked it up. I withdrew the writing implement.

When I unrolled the parchment, I saw that my vow was already written in dark ink.

"Sign beneath." Artemis smiled, her gaze glinting. Clearly, she was already imagining what she'd have me hunt down.

I sucked in a deep breath, ignored Ares's worried gaze, and scrawled my signature on the parchment. I expected to have my voice sucked out of me, just like in *The Little Mermaid* when Ariel had signed her voice over to Ursula, the Sea Witch.

Well, this was a first. A blood oath to a god.

Oh, I was in over my head.

CHAPTER SIX

I handed the parchment back to Artemis, which she took with a satisfied smile, then I pulled the mirror from my pocket. Breath held, I looked.

My heart dropped. "Shit. The sky is dark."

"He's close," Ares said.

"Very."

"Come." Artemis waved us forward. "There's no time to waste. We must beat him to the Tower of Athena."

My gaze darted to hers. "You're helping us?"

"I want my favor."

I grinned. "Then, by all means."

She turned and strode to her horse, waving her hand to make the parchment disappear. Then she vaulted onto her stallion and cantered out of the temple. Ares and I ran to catch up.

We sprinted out onto the main entrance steps. Two large black horses waited just at the edge of the steps. I climbed into the saddle of the nearest one and followed Artemis. Ares followed, an expert rider. I held on for dear life as we galloped between the trees. Large birds fluttered around us, escorting us to the border. They reminded me of Jeff.

Where was he, anyway? Normally, the little dragon would be here for this kind of thing.

"We're not far, now!" Artemis called back.

The trees began to thin, marking the edge of her territory, I had to assume. The sky began to darken quickly. Magically. I could almost feel the evil crackle of Drakon's magic.

By the time the trees gave way to open field, the sky was almost pitch-black. An unnatural glow illuminated a dark tower on top of a hill, about three hundred yards in the distance.

"The Tower of Athena," Artemis yelled back. "Be ready for anything."

Since this was the gods' last shot at protecting the stone from Drakon, it had to be good.

Tension prickled my skin as I galloped across the field, waiting for whatever Athena would send at us.

When low, deep growls sounded around me, I shivered.

The beasts charged out of the dark, monsters the size of cows but with the bodies of giant bulldogs. Except that there was nothing cute and doglike about them. Their heads were skeletons, with huge horns and fangs that looked like they could tear through flesh in an instant. Scales covered their bulky bodies, and their feet were tipped with talons that dug into the earth as they hurtled toward us from a hundred yards away.

"Athena's beasts of war," Artemis cried. "Only iron arrows will defeat them."

Artemis raised her bow, firing in quick succession at the nearest beast. It took three arrows to fell the creature, which finally tripped and tumbled to the ground.

I conjured my bow, along with an iron arrow. The material felt strange in my hand as I fired. It flew toward a hound that was only fifty yards away, sinking into its leg. The beast hissed like a giant snake, but kept coming. I fired again and again, finally taking it out when it was only twenty yards from me. I could make out the black flame of its eyes as it fell. Could feel the dark stain of its magic and its desire to tear me limb from limb.

The three of us galloped across the field, the thundering hoof beats unable to drown out the snarls of the beasts of war. Artemis fired her arrows like the goddess she was, with deadly precision and speed that made my head spin. I tried to keep up, but managed to fell only one beast for every three that she took out.

When a beast got past our arrows, heading straight for Ares, he drew his shadow sword and leaned over, slicing cleanly through the neck of the galloping creature. The skull tumbled to the ground.

Bad-ass. Apparently they could be felled by iron arrows *and* shadow swords. What couldn't that thing cut through?

Ares galloped ahead, directing his horse toward a cluster of beasts that raced toward us. His sword sliced through the air so quickly it looked like a blur. Skulls tumbled to the ground as he decapitated the beasts.

I fired three arrows at once, taking out a monster that was nearly upon me.

"There!" Ares pointed to the top of the tower. It glowed with a pale white light.

The stone of Synnaroe.

We were still a hundred and fifty yards away when the first burst of lightning cracked in the air. My heart jumped.

Drakon!

He was supposed to arrive when the lightning lit the sky.

"Go!" I cried, nudging my horse to go faster. He galloped across the plain, nearly flying.

Up ahead, a dark shadow stretched across the ground.

"Slow!" Artemis cried. "There is a crevasse."

She was right. I was only thirty yards from it now, and could make out the breadth—too far to jump—and depth—probably deep enough to kill me.

A horrible shriek rent the night air.

I looked up. In the distance, Drakon appeared, flying toward the tower. He was massive, his wings the color of coal, and flying so fast that I'd never catch him on my horse. The crevasse wouldn't stop him.

Lightning struck, illuminating his terrifying figure.

The difference between him and me was so clear in that moment.

Dismay gouged at my chest.

How would I get across the crevasse?

This was when I needed Jeff.

A flash of red and green appeared out of the corner of my eye. Jeff!

As if he'd heard me, he appeared. But he was bigger. So much bigger. At least thirty feet long. So that was what he'd been doing all this time—growing.

My heart leapt as he flew toward me, red wings raking the air. He screeched, a joyous sound, and flew alongside my galloping horse.

Without stopping to analyze, I scrambled up into a crouch on the saddle, and then leapt onto Jeff's back. I clung to him, gripping the rigid spines on his back. He screeched and wheeled away from the horse, headed straight for Drakon.

Wind tore at my hair as I adjusted my seat, getting a good grip. This was nothing like riding a horse or even a griffon. Jeff's massive wings whooshed through the air. Joy and terror made my heart thunder.

"Get under him!" I called.

Jeff blew a massive blast of fire and flew faster toward Drakon. My enemy was close to the tower now, only fifty yards away. We were twenty from him, but Jeff's determination made him fast.

I drew my sword from the ether, a trick that Ares had taught me, and gripped it. I had one chance. I didn't think I'd hit his heart last time. This time, my aim needed to be true.

The tower loomed as we neared, the stone shining bright and white from its perch at the top. Lightning struck all around, the thunder deafening.

As we neared Drakon, Jeff blew a blast of fire at his tail. The bright orange flames lit up the night, singeing Drakon.

The shadow dragon didn't even notice.

But his attention was fully on the stone. I could almost feel his greed, just under the surface of the dark magic that radiated from him, sickening me.

"Lower," I called to Jeff.

He darted beneath Drakon, then rose up. I squinted, searching for his black heart. There, in the middle of his chest, glowing black.

I lunged up with my sword, striking hard.

It sank into his chest, but he shrieked and swooped away.

Damn it.

Not a direct hit.

He whirled around, his black gaze on me. Debating.

Would he strike?

He turned, flying for the tower. His goal was the stone, and he wouldn't be diverted.

"One more try, Jeff! Be fast!"

Jeff burst forward. I clung to his back, the wind ripping at my hair, as he darted under Drakon and shot upward. The massive black dragon blocked out the dark sky. My heart thundered as I rose up on Jeff's back. My focus zeroed in on Drakon's heart.

I struck, stabbing my blade through his shadowy form until the tip of my sword pierced him straight in the heart. For the briefest second, I could see it so clearly that I could taste the victory.

Then an electric shock darted down the blade and into me, sending pain tearing through my muscles and bones. Drakon thrashed in the air, roaring loud enough to shake my brain in my skull. He thrashed, one of his massive wings knocking into Jeff. The same electric current shot through my dragon.

Jeff shrieked, the blow sending him pinwheeling in the air.

My muscles had turned to jelly and my mind to mush. I could barely hang on to Jeff. We fell, plummeting toward the ground, wind tearing at my clothes and hair, roaring through my head. At some point, I must have let go. We fell side by side, but the drop was short.

I slammed into the ground, pain flaring through my back.

Hazily, I blinked, turning my head and searching for Jeff. For Drakon.

Jeff lay near me, limp on the ground. Slowly, he raised his head. I clung to that, desperate to take it as a good sign.

Fifty yards in the distance, at the base of the tower, Drakon lay in a lump.

My heart leapt. Was he dead?

But the great black dragon shuddered and rose. He crawled the last few yards to the base of the tower, using his massive wings like limbs. He was evil personified, his eyes blazing with dark light.

Then he began to climb the tower, a dragon version of King Kong. Great claws at the tips of his wings plunged into the tower stone as he dragged himself up.

"No!" I scrambled unsteadily to my feet, my muscles screaming.

"Nix!" Ares's shout sounded from behind me.

I turned. He galloped toward me, leaning over the side of his saddle. He must have found a bridge over the crevasse! I reached up and he grabbed me, swinging me onto the horse behind him. I landed on the horse, clinging to Ares, and he galloped faster, headed straight for the tower.

I had no idea what we'd do when we reached it, but *something*.

Except that Drakon was nearly at the top now, his great body clawing up the dark stone. He scrambled through the great windows that glowed from the stone.

"No!" I could just barely see him wrap his huge body around the glowing light until it was extinguished completely.

Then he disappeared.

Gone.

Frustration tore through me. Failure. I wanted to scream, beat at the earth. Have a tantrum of epic proportions.

It was Jeff, and worry over him that saved me from doing that. As Ares slowed the stallion to a halt, I turned to look back at my dragon. He was sitting upright now, smaller than he had been. Only the size of a very large cow. He shook his head, wobbly.

I collapsed against Ares's back, gratitude welling in me. But failure was hot on its heels. Worry and grief, too.

"We failed," I said.

"Just this time."

I nodded, my mind racing. What would we do from here? What was our next move supposed to be?

Galloping hoof beats sounded from behind us. I turned. Artemis rode toward us, her blond hair whipping in the wind. She stopped her horse near us.

"Your bravery was commendable," she said.

"I've failed."

"But not permanently." She glanced around, her gaze landing on the bodies of the fallen beasts of war. "I must go. Athena may not like that I was here. But when this is over, I will come to you for my tribute."

"All right. Thank you for your help."

She nodded, her silver eyes serious, then turned her horse and galloped back, aiming for a section of land bridge that would take her over the crevasse. That must have been the way Ares had come for me.

I turned back to Ares. "What now?"

"Home. Then we come up with another plan."

It was all there was left to do, really.

A woman's voice sounded from nearby. "I must say, I'd hoped you'd stop him."

I turned toward the tower, catching sight of a figure striding toward us. A woman with dark hair, serious gray eyes, and wearing ancient Greek armor. A white owl perched on her shoulder. Her magic was like a one-two punch to the gut. A feeling of both calm and chaos, the sound of battle, the smell of blood. But also the comforting sense of knowing what to do in a bad situation.

"Athena," I said. "Goddess of wisdom and war."

She inclined her head.

"I'm sorry about your beasts of war," I said.

She stopped about a dozen feet from us. "They will regenerate. As for you ... You were lucky to survive this."

With every muscle aching from the electric shock and my bones feeling jolted to the marrow, I had to agree. Whether I'd survive my next encounter with Drakon? That was yet to be determined.

"Do you know why my blade didn't kill Drakon?" I asked the question that had been lurking in my mind. "I hit him right in the heart. I saw it."

She nodded, lips pursed. "Only the beak of the phoenix can kill Drakon."

"What does that mean?" I didn't have a beak. Was it figurative?

"Only you can determine that. And before you ever get that far, you will have to work on your flaws."

"Flaws?" Didn't love the sound of that, even though it was likely true.

"Yes. Your greatest flaw is lack of belief in yourself. It has colored your experiences here and in the mortal world. But it needs to stop. You've proven yourself here, today. Your kindness in helping Nestor, your bravery in defeating the beasts of war. You *are* worthy, Phoenix Knight, and you will need that knowledge and strength of will to carry you through to the end of this journey. You will not survive if you doubt yourself."

So I might survive. That was good news. "I'd never realized I doubted myself so much. I really thought I'd been getting a handle on it lately."

"Doubt is an insidious thing, creeping up when we least expect it. Have faith. Pursue your course of action and trust that you are good enough. You've proven it over and over."

Warmth pushed away some of the pain in my muscles. Ares reached back and gripped my hand. I could feel his agreement. It radiated from him like the light of the sun.

His closeness also made me realize that I was still mounted on Artemis's horse. Should I get down to greet the goddess?

I'd probably fall flat on my face. And since she didn't seem to mind...

I stayed seated. In the distance, Jeff wobbled through the air, trying out his wings.

"Will he be all right?" I asked.

"Yes, though that was quite a blow for your familiar."

"He's brave."

"That he is." Athena made a gesture with her hand, then twisted her wrist so her palm faced upward. A white charm lay in her palm. She approached, her magical signature growing stronger with every step.

Frankly, it was damned uncomfortable. Wisdom and war created two very conflicting magical signatures. I sucked in a shallow breath and braced myself, my weak muscles threatening to give up the fight and send me plummeting off the horse's back.

Athena raised her hand, offering the charm to me. My gaze darted to her owl, which watched me with thoughtful golden eyes, and then to the charm.

"What is it?" I asked, remembering all the tales of tricky gods.

Athena, for all her wisdom and power, had also been the one to smite Medusa. She was dangerous.

"A gift. Freely given, which I am not always wont to do." Her steady gray eyes met mine. "But you will need it, Phoenix. Very soon. You came here today and did not get what you wanted. But I hope you will get what you need. This charm is a temporary gift of wisdom and mental clarity. You will know when to use it— when your sisters are near—and it will make all the difference."

Well, I couldn't look that gift horse in the mouth. "Thank you."

I reached for the charm. It tingled coolly against my fingertips as I plucked it from her palm.

"When you have defeated Drakon, which I hope desperately that you do, return the stone to me," she said.

"Of course."

"I will send you home now. You don't have time to make your way back through the Underworld."

"Nor the strength."

Athena's eyes traveled to Ares. "You have been quiet, vampire."

"It's not really my show, is it?" Ares said. "I'm the backup."

"Phoenix will not be able to accomplish this without you. Or without her family and friends. Your strength is in your bond. In your unity. Don't forget that."

I swallowed hard, hating to hear that. I didn't want to put any of them at risk. But she was right. If today had proven anything, I wasn't nearly strong enough on my own to defeat Drakon.

CHAPTER SEVEN

Athena sent Ares and me back to Magic's Bend with a flick of her wrist. Magic swirled around us and sucked us through the ether. It was dark when we arrived back in Magic's Bend. The moon was out and the streetlights on. What time it was, I had no idea. I'd lost all track.

Cold wind cut across my cheeks, stinging my eyes. I sighed. This had been one long winter. I hoped I'd be welcoming spring with Drakon and the Triumvirate duties behind me.

Then my *deirfiúr* and I would be safe and free.

I held on to Ares for support—my muscles still felt like noodles—and turned to inspect the street. We were in front of P & P. The lights within glowed warm and welcoming. It was empty other than Cass, Del, Aidan, and Roarke, with Connor behind the bar. The little sign on the door was flipped to CLOSED.

"Perfect timing," I said. My stomach grumbled as if it agreed.

Ares grinned, then wrapped an arm around my waist and helped me inside. The door wasn't locked, so we let ourselves into the warmth. The scent of coffee and pastries made my mouth water.

"Nix!" Cass stood.

Del joined her. "You look like hell."

I laughed, but stopped short when the movement made my chest hurt. "I'm good." My gaze landed on Jeff, who already sat in one of the chairs. He was small again, and an empty glass of whiskey sat in front of him. There was a bottle of Dr. Pepper next to it. Apparently he was expanding his tastes. "When did he get here?"

"Just a couple minutes ago." Aidan grinned, his auburn hair glinting in the light. "He went straight for my whiskey, so I gave it to him. Then he pulled a bottle of soda from the fridge."

The little dragon burped, looking content. At least he was getting better.

Ares helped me stagger to the chairs.

"Coffee and food coming right up. Leftovers from the day all right?" Connor called from behind the counter.

My stomach grumbled. "Amazing."

"Thanks." Ares smiled at him, then helped me sit.

"Are you okay?" Cass's concerned eyes met mine. "You really do look pretty rough."

"Yeah, I'll be okay. How did it go with looking for the dragons?"

"Aren't you going to tell us about the stone and Drakon?" Del asked. "We've been on the edge of our seats."

"I failed. And I will tell you. But first, I have to know how you did. Any luck?" It was our only hope, now.

"Maybe," Cass said. "We went to the tallest mountain in Norway, as Hildr the Valkyrie told us to. It's located in the central part of the country."

"But there were definitely no dragons there," Del said. "Just a ski resort full of humans and a few supernaturals."

Shit. "A *ski resort?*"

"Dragons wouldn't be sleeping beneath a ski resort," Ares said.

"No kidding." Del nodded. "But while we were poking around, this strange old woman came up to us. Her magic was different. Unidentifiable. And she said, 'This is not what you seek, for it is not on this land.'"

"And then she freaking disappeared." Cass threw her hands up.

I scowled, trying to piece it all together. "But you're certain she recognized you somehow? Or knew what you were there for?"

"Yes." Cass nodded emphatically. "She reminded me a bit of Hildr. Just much older. And wearing a fluffy black parka."

Del passed me her phone. I took it and looked at the screen. It was a photo of an older woman's side profile. She wore a bright pink jacket and had a cloud of white hair. Her gaze was serious. There was something special about her.

"Hmm. Old ladies are now giving us clues." I leaned back in my chair. That was actually a good thing, since old ladies were just young ladies who'd seen and done more stuff. Which made her message more likely to be legit.

Connor approached with coffee and food. I took my plate and cup, then shot him a grateful glance. Right now, he was my savior. "Thank you."

Ares repeated the sentiment.

"Anytime, guys." Connor grinned and went back to the counter, clearly keeping an ear perked. Which was fine by me, since he'd probably be jumping into this with us soon enough.

I bit into the pasty—a regular beef and potato one, which tasted divine right now—and studied the picture of the old woman. "You said that she told you that what we seek is not on this land?"

Cass nodded.

"Strange choice of words," Ares said.

"Yeah." There was something there—a connection my mind wasn't making. Hidlr had definitely said the largest mountain in Norway. Yet this woman said differently.

So what was the deal?

As I chewed and swallowed my pasty, I remembered the charm that Athena had given me. This was the moment. She'd said it would come soon and that I'd be with my sisters, as she'd called them. I needed clarity of thought. Wisdom. A mental jolt of Adderall or something.

And I could just feel that the information was here, buried in this woman's message.

I reached into my pocket and withdrew the ivory charm.

"What's that?" Cass asked.

"Gift from Athena. For wisdom." I clutched it in my hand, asking the magic to help me. As if it understood, it flared bright, light shining between my fingers. For the briefest moment, my mind felt clear. Like I could understand everything that happened and all the connections in the world.

Oddly, the first thing my brain latched onto was Ares. Every moment of our time together played in my head, so fast it was over in a flash. But it all made sense. Though it'd been such a short time, loving him was so honest and so right. Any fear I'd had about my feelings being from our blood bond had been banished last week—but this just cemented it even more in my mind.

I forced my thoughts from Ares and to the dragons. To what Hildr had told us, and then what the strange old woman had said.

"Oh!" I gasped. "The tallest mountain in Norway is not on the mainland. It's hidden from all eyes and has never been charted by topographers."

"Where is it?" Ares asked.

"Svalbard."

"Where the hell is that?" Cass asked.

"It's an island, north of Norway, far into the Arctic Sea. A territory of theirs."

Del leaned back in her seat, a smile on her face. "Of course. That makes perfect sense. Norway is remote, but not remote enough for dragons. And that's what the old woman meant when she said 'not on this land.' It's in Norway, just not on the mainland."

I smiled, a bit of hope finally rising within me. Athena's charm had already faded in my hand, the magic extinguished. I let out a shaky breath. That had been a wild trip.

"So now we know where the dragons are," Cass said. "Roughly. What happened with Drakon?"

I frowned. "It didn't go well. He got the battery, which I'm sure you assumed. And I can't kill him with my sword—not even with a direct blow to the heart."

It'd been my last hope. At least, the last idea I actually had.

"So that's why you want to know if we found the dragons," Del said. "We have to bring the fight to him."

"Exactly. He can't use his spell without a FireSoul conduit. We are his ideal conduits. Without us, he can't do anything."

"Doesn't that mean you should stay away from him?" Roarke asked.

I nodded. "Yes, ideally. But we can't sit back from the fight. I am the only one who can defeat him, and Athena made it clear that I can't do it without my *deirfiúr* or Ares. If we wait too long, avoiding him in hopes that he won't go through with his plan without us, he'll likely settle for another FireSoul to use as a conduit. Maybe more than one."

"So you three being his chosen FireSouls might buy us a couple days to come up with a plan," Ares said. "But in the end, you will have to face him."

"I think so." I downed the rest of my coffee in two gulps. "Which means finding the dragons and figuring out a way to stop Drakon."

"We're bringing the fight to him," Cass said.

"Better to be on the offensive anyway," Del added.

I nodded, pleased to see that Ares, Aidan, and Roarke seemed to agree. Jeff, for his part, was already asleep.

I set my cup down and pulled the mirror that Pan had given

me from my pocket, hoping that I could see Drakon. It was blank —just a regular mirror again. Even though I couldn't see Drakon, I had to imagine that after our battle, he was resting and recovering.

Which was what we needed to do, as well.

~

After finishing our drinks, we all agreed to get a good night's sleep. No way I'd be able to trek through Svalbard in my current condition.

When Ares helped me rise, that became all the more apparent. I could barely walk.

"Drakon really did a number on me," I said. "If I thought his touch was electric, stabbing a blade into his heart is a whole new level."

Ares wrapped an arm around my waist and helped me through the door of P & P. Jeff had decided to sleep it off in P & P, and everyone else was staying a few more minutes, so we had the quiet street to ourselves as we walked.

I couldn't help but think of what we'd just been through—my injuries made it impossible to forget.

"Had I even been close to stopping Drakon back there?" I said.

"Perhaps not," Ares said. "Our best chance was beating him to the stone and stealing it to hide it. Once he appeared on the field, our odds were dismal."

"I wounded him, at least."

"And learned plenty in the process." He squeezed me lightly around the waist. "And not just from the wisdom charm that Athena gave you."

"You mean, believing in myself?"

"That too."

I sighed. "An important lesson." If anything, I was going to force myself to take something positive from the failure with

Drakon. It was another stepping stone closer to defeating him. Sure, I'd wanted to end it there. But we didn't always get what we wanted. "Hey, when Athena said that sometimes we get what we need, not what we want, do you think she was singing that Stones song in her head?"

Ares chuckled. "Maybe. But somehow I doubt it."

I laughed, enjoying the quiet moment beneath the stars. It was a rare, clear-skied winter night. Despite the golden streetlights, I could still see the stars above. It was dark inside Ancient Magic, and I wished the shop were open.

It would be. It had to be.

Because now, more than ever, we were closer to defeating Drakon. And with my friends' help, we had a chance.

I opened the green door to our building and wearily made my way up the stairs. Halfway up, Ares swooped me up into his arms.

"Hey, I can walk."

"Not easily." He pressed a kiss to my forehead.

"Clearly not." I leaned my head against his shoulder, reliving the moment when he'd told me he loved me. That had *really* happened.

Ares let us into my apartment and sat me on the couch. I pulled him down next to me, my muscles trembling from the strain.

He turned to me, clearly about to say something, but I spoke first. "Could you heal me?"

The corner of his mouth kicked up. "I was just about to ask. But it's rare that you're the one requesting."

I shrugged. "I'm not worried about the blood bond anymore."

He pressed a kiss to my forehead, then pulled back and raised his wrist to his mouth. His white fangs descended, then punctured the skin. I shivered.

He held his arm up to my lips, and I took his forearm in my hands. Trembling, I pressed my lips against his skin, drawing deep of his blood. Flavor exploded over my tongue, strange and

78

delicious. Warmth flowed through me, strengthening my muscles and calming my mind.

Pleasure followed, so acute that I moaned, my eyes fluttering shut.

Ares withdrew his arm. It took all I had not to yank it back. I opened my eyes in time to see him raise his wrist and swipe his tongue over the wounds, closing them. Heat streaked through me.

I lunged for him, straddling his waist and wrapping my arms around his neck. I pressed my mouth to his, kissing him ferociously.

It felt *amazing*.

I didn't know if it was his blood, our declarations, or some combination of the two, but I was on fire. I rubbed against him, desperate to get as close as I could. His strong arms wrapped around me, squeezing me tight before he withdrew.

I was about to complain when I felt his big hands running down my sides and up my back, as if he couldn't get enough of me. It was mutual. I touched him everywhere I could reach, images of tearing his clothes off racing through my mind.

But another thought blared stronger than all the rest, brought on by desire. Need.

"Bite me," I said.

"What?" He pulled back, eyes heavy-lidded and hot.

"I mean it. I want it." And I did. Badly. It was supposed to feel good—and what a bond it would be … "Do it."

He didn't hesitate. It was as if something had snapped his iron control. Maybe it had been my determination that had done it, but I didn't care enough to figure it out now. Not when Ares was lowering his head to my neck.

Excitement raced through me, followed by a sharp, small stab of pain. It was gone in a flash, followed by heat and pleasure. Ares's mouth felt like silk.

I shuddered against him, letting the ecstasy flow through me, coil tight within me. He groaned low against my throat, the vibrations sending another jolt of pleasure through me.

When he withdrew his mouth, I wanted to yank him back toward me. But the swipe of his hot tongue against the wounds at my throat sent another jolt of pleasure through me.

I moaned, my head tilting back.

Ares swept me up in his arms, then headed for the bedroom.

CHAPTER EIGHT

The next morning, I kissed Ares goodbye at my front door.

"Thanks for last night," I said.

He grinned. "Likewise."

I shivered, then shoved away the thoughts and focused on the work to be done. "How long will you be in the Vampire Realm?"

"A few hours at most. I'll try to coordinate backup for a future fight against Drakon, then I can meet you back here."

"Good. Thank you. We'll need all the help we can get."

I gave Ares one last kiss, pressing my lips hard to his, then turned and headed for Del's apartment. Ares followed me down the steps, then disappeared out into the cool morning air as I stopped and knocked on Del's door.

She yanked it open immediately. "Good timing. As it turns out, Svalbard isn't just a chunk of rock in the middle of the ocean. It's a magical chunk of rock with a super magical mountain. And that makes it a pain in the ass to find."

"What do you mean?" I'd planned to meet Cass and Del to hunt for the location of the mountain, but it sounded like she'd already gotten started.

"There's no mention of a super tall mountain on Svalbard

anywhere on the internet. As far as the modern world is concerned, Svalbard exists. But it doesn't contain the largest mountain in Norway."

"So we're going to check your trove?" Del's trove contained an enormous collection of books and a few old maps.

"That's the plan. Cass is already in there. Ready to dive into the dust?"

"You betcha."

I followed her back through her bedroom and into her crowded trove. Piles of books formed towers all around us, and though she'd mentioned dust, there was none to be found. Though her organizational system was weird, she kept the place spotless.

We joined Cass in the back near a massive pile of leather-bound tomes and got to work, leafing through pages. I moved as quickly as I could, searching for any reference that could help us. But two hours later, surrounded by an ever growing pile of books and scrolls, we were still coming up empty.

"The mountain isn't on any map." Del shifted set down a map and sighed. "I've checked them all."

"All of these books are coming up empty." I frowned.

"So if the internet has nothing and your trove has nothing, we'll need to go farther afield," Cass said.

"Dr. Garriso and the fae Fiona," I said. Our friend at the Museum for Magical History and the fae librarian were the two most knowledgeable people we knew. Their libraries and memories far surpassed ours. I looked at Cass and Del. "I'll start with Dr. Garriso if you'll contact Fiona."

"On it," Del said.

Cass saluted.

We left the trove, filing into Del's bedroom. They stayed behind, and I took the stairs two at a time to my apartment, grabbed the keys to Fabio, then headed down to the street. The late winter sun was just rising when I stepped out into the chill air.

Fabio was parked just down the street. It didn't take me long to reach the Museum for Magical History. Despite the early hour, Dr. Garriso was sure to be there. We were pretty sure he even slept there occasionally, so dedicated was he to his passion.

I parked in the lot behind the museum and hurried toward the back door. I tapped on Dr. Garriso's office window to alert him, then knocked on the unassuming entrance that led to the staff offices.

A few moments later, Dr. Garriso opened the door. He was in his seventies, with flyaway white hair and a tweed coat that looked very Sherlock Holmes on him. It suited the old scholar.

"Come in, come in." He gestured me inside the barren hallway.

Though the main part of the museum was a beautifully decorated old building, the staff offices were located off a linoleum-tiled hallway in the basement. Fluorescent lights buzzed in the ceiling.

"Whatever you're here about, it must be important," Dr. Garriso said.

"How'd you guess?"

"I've been getting a fair number of difficult questions from your camp lately." He grinned. "I just hope I can help with this one."

"Me too."

Dr. Garriso led me down the hall to his office. Stepping inside was like going to another world. The twentieth century office drudgery of the hall gave way to a book-lined office that looked straight out of a nineteenth century lord's manor. Floor-to-ceiling shelves were filled with leather-bound books. Tiffany lamps cast a warm glow over the dark furniture and heavy desk.

"Tea?" Dr. Garriso asked.

I smiled. It wouldn't matter if the world were ending—Dr.

Garriso would always offer tea. "Thank you, but I'm not sure I have the time."

Concern wrinkled his brow. "Yes, yes. Of course."

I took a seat in one of the leather chairs at the end of the narrow room.

He sat next to me and leaned forward. "What is it that I can help you with?"

I told him about Svalbard and the mountain that couldn't be found on any maps.

Interest gleamed in his eyes, and he tapped his chin. "Interesting. Very interesting. I think I may know just what you're talking about."

I opened my mouth to ask what he meant, but he leapt up, as spry as a man in his twenties, and hurried to the far wall. He scaled a wooden ladder and reached for a large, dusty book.

"I've always been interested in the ancient religions," he said as he hurried back. "The problem is that there is usually so little written history. And what we have isn't necessarily reliable. Some things weren't written down until hundreds of years after the fact, and how are we supposed to know what got lost in the process?"

"So you think this has something to do with an ancient religion?"

"It just might." He sat and opened the huge book. A small poof of dust plumed upward. Quickly, he skimmed through the pages. Then he stopped, pointing to one. "Yes, yes. Here it is. There is mention of primordial gods in Northern Europe. The first gods, who came long before the Greek or the Celtic or the Norse. The primordial gods."

"I've never heard of them."

"Not many people have. But the Icelandic poet Snorri Sturleson recorded an ancient tale, passed down through the centuries, of a land of ice and snow that was protected by the primordial gods."

"I'll bet twenty bucks it was Svalbard."

"Yes, very likely. It was said to be an island, far off the coast, where the polar bears were larger than houses."

Ehhh. I grimaced. "If it's protected by the primordial gods, that could mean it's hidden from human eyes, right?"

"Yes. And your giant mountain would be hidden as well."

"So how do I reach it?"

He leaned over the page, brow drawn. After a moment, he spoke. "It says here that there is an entry in Heimsrkingla. There's nothing there now—just rocks and snow on Norway's northernmost coast. But you should go and see if you can trigger the magic."

"What kind of trigger?" I thought of the dwarves in Norway and how we'd had to trigger Sven's magic with the amber stone.

"I have a feeling that if this is what I think it is—and you are who we all think you are—that you won't need to do anything other than show up."

"I hope you're right."

His gaze turned grave. "So do I. Because you need to succeed, Nix. And I've just given you all the information that I know."

"Thank you."

He grinned. "My pleasure. Not every day that my knowledge is put to such world-saving use."

World-saving. "I just hope I can live up to that."

I arrived back at Factory Row the same time Ares did. He strode down the sidewalk toward me and pulled me in for a kiss. My mind spun for the briefest second, every inch of me focusing on his touch, before he drew away.

I wobbled a bit, steadied my breathing—and then remembered everything that faced us. That sobered me right up.

"Did you find anything?" he asked.

"Yeah. You?"

"Yes. Should we need them, I have a contingent of vampire soldiers who will help us with the fight."

I grinned. "Thank you. And I got lucky, though Cass and Del struck out."

"You know where to go?"

"I do."

"Good. Because there's a crowd waiting." He pointed behind me.

I turned, looking through the window of P & P. I'd only had eyes for Ares when he'd arrived and hadn't noticed how many people were inside.

Cass and Del, with Aidan and Roarke. Along with Connor, Claire, Aerdeca, Mordaca, Bree, and Ana.

I gave Ares a quizzical look. He shrugged, which I should have expected. How would he know their intentions better than I?

"Let's go figure this out, then." I walked into the warmth of P & P and looked at all of the people. "So, guys, what's the party for?"

"We were hoping you'd tell us." Aerdeca tapped her fingers on her chair arm. She was dressed in her tactical fight wear instead of her usual white pantsuit. So was Mordaca.

"Yes, Cass says that you've found the dragons," Mordaca said.

"*Maybe* found the dragons," Cass said.

Mordaca waved her black-clawed fingers. "Whatever."

I approached the group. "Yes, there is a chance I have found the dragons, but I can't guarantee it. Why are you here, though?"

"To help you, obviously." Bree flicked her dark hair back from her face.

"We barely know you," I said. "Not that I don't appreciate the help, but you're risking a lot for people you barely know."

"We're risking a lot because there's a lot at stake," Ana said. "All the magic in the world. That means our magic, too. And the magic of every innocent supernatural out there."

"And we're not interested in running from a fight," Bree said.

A smile twitched at my lips. "I've gotten that impression." I looked at Aerdeca and Mordaca. "Same goes for you?"

"We've known what was at stake from the moment we touched the beaker," Aerdeca said. "We're here to fight."

I glanced at Connor and Claire, but their faces basically said, "Give me a break."

I didn't bother asking them why they had our backs. They *always* had our backs.

"All right, then," I said. "We do need your help. Normally, we'd take fewer people on recon—which is what this will be—but we can't afford for Del, Cass, or me to get caught by Drakon."

"So we'll be your guards." Bree cracked her knuckles and grinned.

"Yeah, basically." We could protect ourselves normally. But this wasn't normal.

"With this crowd, I think we're going in loaded for bear," Cass said.

I grimaced. "Good, because there will be polar bears. Big ones."

"So we're headed north?" Del asked.

"Yes." I relayed Dr. Garriso's information about the primordial gods and what we might face.

We didn't have much of a plan other than show up, stick together, and hope for the best. We were really walking into the unknown.

"This is some serious chosen-one business going on," Bree muttered.

She was right. And whoever had done the choosing—I sure hoped they knew what they were doing.

~

With Ares, Cass, and Mordaca as the transporters in the group, it didn't take long to transport everyone to Heimsrkingla. After everyone had gotten into winter clothes, Ares took me first so that we could scout out the terrain. Everyone else followed behind.

As soon as I arrived on the far northern coast of Norway, cold wind whipped across my cheeks, making my eyes water. Every bit of land that wasn't barren rock was covered by snow. The black sea roiled, whitecaps topping the waves.

It was much colder than the fjord had been, and much more desolate. Especially in the dark. Damned winter. It seemed that most of our time in Norway would be spent in the dark. Especially this far north, where there would be no sun all month. At least there was a bright moon and stars. Reflection off the snow gave plenty of light.

I spun in a circle, taking it all in. Mountains rose high behind me. At the sea, small islands of rock dotted the landscape.

Close to the water, something pulled at me. Cass had just arrived with Roarke and Del, but I left them behind, crunching through the snow toward the water's edge. It felt like my dragon sense, but I hadn't employed it.

Ares joined me. "Where are you going?"

"I feel something. Magic. It's different." Maybe it was the same thing Dr. Garriso had been speaking of.

I clambered over rocks as waves crashed against the shore. The magic grew stronger, sparking on the air.

"Do you feel that?" I asked.

"Nothing," Ares said.

Hmmm. I quickened my pace, my heart racing as I neared the magic. At the shore, there was a barren spot with no snow. It was a large flat rock, about ten feet wide. I walked out to the middle of it, magic singing up through my bones.

There was a carving on the rock, a large swirl. As soon as I stepped into the middle, the magic swelled.

Water splashed.

I looked up.

A large ship was rising up from the sea.

"Holy fates," the murmur sounded from behind me. Other exclamations followed.

Water poured off the rigging and deck. It glittered in the moonlight, a structure made entirely of ice. It was clear in parts and cloudy in others, but the whole thing was definitely made of ice.

These Norwegian Vikings sure did like their boats.

Bree stepped up beside me, her dark hair hidden behind her hood. Her voice was filled with awe. "Skithblathnir, the ship of the gods."

"What is it?"

"The best ship ever built, according to Norse mythology."

My gaze traveled over the ship. It was huge, with the sleek lines of a Viking warship. But there were no shields at the waterline, which a warship would likely have. There were also no sailors.

"I think we're supposed to board," Ares said.

I nodded slowly, still awed.

"Pretty impressive," Mordaca said. "Yes. I'd say you are the chosen one."

I let out a shuddery breath. "Then let's board."

I made my way to the shore. There was either deep water or magic right here, because the ship lined up exactly with the rocks near the water. I jumped from one of the rocks onto the deck. Despite being made of ice, it wasn't slippery underfoot, thank fates.

Ares followed, then Del and Cass. Everyone else boarded afterward.

"Anyone else think it's a tad risky to board a boat that is technically made of water?" Claire asked.

"Yes." I nodded emphatically. Water on top of water. We'd just have to hope it didn't melt.

Once everyone was on board, the boat pulled back from the shore, then set out to sea.

"There's no sail raised," Cass said.

I looked up at the empty mast. "Nope."

Magic propelled this vessel. I looked at Del, whose dark hair whipped in the wind. "Do you see any ghosts?"

She shook her head. Del was the only one among us who could see ghosts that didn't willingly show themselves.

Ana stepped up to the rail and looked warily into the sea. "Is it a ghost ship if there're no ghosts?"

I frowned. "I don't know. But it sure feels like one."

The ship cut through the waves, which got bigger as we headed farther out into sea. If this was some dark magic, it could take us out and drop us in the middle of the ocean.

The moonlight glittered on the waves as they rose and fell around us. The cold cut through my jacket. I shivered, wrapping my arms more tightly around myself.

"We have to be getting close," Cass said. "This is too wild to not be the right track."

I had to agree with her logic. The crazier and more magical things got, the more I thought we were going in the right direction.

It felt like hours that we sailed, the wind chilling our bones and muscles. In the distance, storm clouds rolled and lightning struck. Eventually, snow began to fall, the clouds blocking out the light of the moon. It was so dark it was hard to see the ocean now, and claustrophobia pressed in on me.

Finally, the snow stopped. The clouds parted and moonlight revealed glowing, snow-covered mountains in the distance.

"That's it." I grinned.

"You feel that, though?" Cass asked.

"Not good," Mordaca murmured.

Aerdeca shook her head in agreement.

They were right. Magic rolled off the land, a threatening electricity in the air. I shivered and tried to ignore it as the boat carried us to the shore. It glided to a stop, and we jumped off one by one, landing in the soft snow. It covered the ground, fluffy and white and so pure it seemed like no one had stepped on it in centuries.

Warily, I walked forward. I was about to call on my dragon sense when figures stepped out of the darkness ahead of us.

They were shrouded in gray robes. Wind flickered, blowing the fabric back and revealing icy forms.

"They're not human," Del whispered.

"Nope." They were made of ice, just like the ship.

They stalked toward us, their flowing robes unable to conceal the rigid movements of their icy forms.

I stepped forward. "Hello. I am—"

They gestured, cutting off my words.

Well, okay. That was pretty clear. I looked at my friends. Most shrugged and nodded, which was about how I felt too.

The figures waved us forward, then turned and walked slowly away. We obeyed, tromping through the snow after them. They didn't lead us far, just a few dozen yards to where four large sleighs waited. Each was oversized and pulled by a massive polar bear.

One of the bear's nostrils quivered, then his big head swung around, and he pierced me with cunning black eyes. He roared, the sound shaking snow from a nearby tree.

I stiffened, heart leaping into my throat.

One of the cloaked figures held up a hand, his cloak waving in the breeze. The bear abruptly quieted, but continued to glare at me.

"Without those guys in cloaks, we'd be bear kibble," Cass whispered.

"Yep." I shuddered and climbed into one of the carriages. It, too, was built of ice. Warily, I sat on the bench, waiting for it to melt against my butt.

When it didn't, I relaxed. Thank fates for magic.

Ares joined me, along with Cass and Aidan. Del and Roarke joined Connor and Claire in a sled, while Aerdeca, Mordaca, Bree, and Ana took the other. The cloaked figures sat in the last.

No one said a word, but somehow the bears knew to leave. They lumbered through the snow, effortlessly pulling our carriages.

"This is amazing and terrifying," Cass said.

"Yep. If it weren't for the creepy magic and the icy grim reapers, it'd be a winter fairy tale." I looked up at the snow that had begun to fall. The flakes were fat and white, and settled on the bears' thick white coats.

"I had no idea any of this existed," Aidan said.

"I don't think anyone knows," Ares said. "The magic that brought the boat was triggered by Nix. She felt it, but I felt nothing."

"I didn't feel anything either," Cass said.

"Well, I just hope I'm not leading us to our deaths."

The creepy magic grew stronger as the polar bears pulled our sleighs over hills of snow and past a wide, icy river. Heaviness hung over the place, a threatening magic that raised the hair on my arms.

If these were the ancient gods—the primordials—they were the ones that people had been afraid of. They weren't the happy summer gods who brought sunshine and harvest, that was for sure.

As the sleighs glided over the ground, the moon glittered brightly on the snow. Thank fates it was full—we needed all the light we could get in the endless dark of a Svalbard winter. When we crested a large hill, the moon illuminated the scene ahead.

A steep-sided mountain loomed. An icy castle was built into the base, a massive structure that glittered in the moonlight.

"Whoa." I'd seen an ice hotel on TV before. This was nothing like that measly structure. The castle was oversized—like giants would live within.

"That's ten times the size of a normal castle," Ares said.

He was right. The walls had to soar a thousand feet high. The turrets went even higher, ornate structures that pierced the sky like needles.

The polar bears roared and picked up their pace, racing toward the castle at a breakneck speed.

"Like horses heading home," Cass said. "They must want their hay." She hesitated. "Or raw flesh or whatever."

I grimaced, hoping we wouldn't run into the polar bears when they weren't with their creepy tenders.

The eerie magic increased as we neared the castle. It crept over my skin, cold and prickly. Gods always had the strongest magic, but this was off the charts. We weren't even within the castle walls yet, and I already wanted to climb out of my skin.

The bears slowed in front of the castle, drawing to a halt. A huge gate was set into the walls that towered overhead. I tilted my head back and looked up. The floor dropped away from me, and my head spun. I clung to the seat beneath me. *Hello, vertigo.*

In the other sleigh, one of the figures stood and raised an arm. Sparkling light swirled toward the gate, which groaned as it slowly opened. A blast of freezing air rushed out. I huddled against Ares. He wasn't any warmer, but his presence was a comfort.

The bears dragged the sleighs into a massive courtyard. Somehow, the castle felt bigger from inside. Like it was built for giants.

Ah, crap. I really hoped it hadn't been.

In the middle, a huge fountain shot crystal clear water into the air. In this cold, it should have frozen. But then, the rules didn't apply when there was so much magic in the air.

As smoothly as ghosts, the cloaked figures rose and gestured us forward. Silently—this place seemed to demand silence—we rose and followed them through a huge door decorated with swirled silver set into the ice.

The air vibrated as we went into the massive room beyond. The ceiling soared above, so high that eagles could have flown through without a problem.

I leaned toward Ares and whispered, "If this is the only way to get to the mountain of dragons, how did Drakon make it through?"

"That is a very good question." Ares's tone was grim.

We gathered in the middle of the room, which was empty save for a massive ornate ledge on the far wall. When I heard the first thundering footsteps, it dawned on me that the ledge might be a bench.

I straightened my spine and sucked in a breath.

Then the magic came. Dark and cold and roiling like the sea in winter. It brought with it a howling wind, hunger, and grief.

Yes, these were the winter gods. The darkness of the most desolate time of year. I swayed on my feet, trying to resist the crushing sensation. It felt like an avalanche pounding down on me. Out of the corner of my eye, my friends swayed where they stood, each wobbly but determined to hold their stance.

The giants entered one at a time, entering from an archway to the left. The first was built of jagged icicles. Slender and angular, he was at least sixty feet tall. He stalked toward the bench. The face was androgynous, but somehow I knew he identified as male, and that his name was Isedor. I'd have staked my life on it. That was a crazy godly skill, putting your name directly into someone's mind.

Then came a massive man who was tinged vaguely blue. He was the color of a corpse almost, stocky and muscular, with the squashed face that I normally associated with dwarves. But he was far too large. His hair and beard looked to be made of snow, and his clothes were the faded gray of a winter morning. Lyrtjur, was his name. Once again, it blazed in my mind.

The third figure was almost difficult to see. It entered as a breeze carrying snowflakes, a wind that took the shape of a woman with long flowing hair. She was visible from some angles and not from others, depending upon her stride. The personification of a winter wind, if I had to guess. Called Varemar.

They each took a seat on the bench on the far wall. They towered so far over us, and their magic was so strong, that I felt like nothing more than a gnat at their feet.

They had to grant us passage, or we were screwed.

"Who are you?" said Varemar. Like her snowy, ephemeral figure, her voice sounded like a wind whistling through a forest, which should be impossible. But not here.

I stepped forward, muscles trembling from cold and fear. "I am Phoenix Knight. I've come to defeat the evil Drakon."

"Ah, you come at last," said Varemar.

"You're not easy to find."

"Drakon managed," said Isedor, the icicle giant. His voice grated like ice rubbing against gravel.

"He came before me?" My heart thudded.

The pale blue giant nodded. "He passed here three days ago."

I gasped. "You let him through?"

Too late, I realized that my tone sounded like an accusation. The icicle giant surged to his feet, chips of ice breaking off him to crash to the ground.

"I'm sorry. That tone was rude," I said. "Please accept my apologies."

The icicle god threw out his hand, a harsh gesture that sent a blast of freezing wind right at me. It bowled me over, sending me tumbling across the icy ground. I slammed into the wall behind me, my back aching.

Slowly, I dragged myself to my feet, grateful to see that my friends were all still standing. Tension radiated through Ares, but he was keeping it together.

Good. None of us could beat these guys. Not even Ares.

"Enough, Isedor." The blue giant, Lyrtjur, made a calming gesture with one hand.

Isedor grumbled, and then sat.

I walked forward on trembling legs, trying to craft my apology. But the snowy wind god spoke before I could.

"What makes you think we would not allow Drakon through our territory?" Varemar asked.

I stopped next to Ares, dumbstruck. "Well, uh, he's incredibly evil. He's going to awaken the dragons and wreak havoc everywhere. Then he'll steal all the magic from the world."

Sounded like a laundry list of *the worst shit ever* to me.

But the snowy wind god shrugged an ephemeral shoulder. "You assume we don't want Drakon to succeed. Which is quite myopic of you." She turned to the other two gods. "Why is it that humans are always so obsessed with themselves?"

While I could say that the gods gave us a run for our money, I'd better not.

Varemar turned back to me. "Our magic has nothing to do with your magic. All the supernaturals on Earth could lose their powers, and we would be the same as ever. We owe you nothing."

It was easy to assume that they wouldn't just help us for the sake of it, then.

Isedor shifted, his icicles glinting in the light. "And you assume that we like the status quo. We don't. We haven't been worshipped for millennia." He gestured to the empty great hall. "So we sit here, bored. If Drakon succeeds and throws the world into chaos, the old ways might return. Humans will be so fearful that they will look to the supernatural for answers. Perhaps they will even worship us again."

Shit. I had not been anticipating this.

Varemar leaned forward. "So you can see why we are not overly concerned with preventing Drakon from achieving his goals."

"Does that mean you won't allow me to pass?" My heart thundered in my ears.

Varemar sighed, and a gust of snowy wind blew past my cheeks. "That will be up to you. We will allow you to prove your worthiness. If you pass, you may go through. After that, you may enter Svalbard at your will, transporting wherever you like on the island. If you fail to cross—well, it won't matter. You'll be dead."

I wanted to give her a sarcastic thumbs-up. Instead, I just nodded. Worthiness tests were old hat to me now. Bring on the monsters and the acid lakes.

Varemar stood and pointed in front of her. The ground groaned and cracked, opening right in front of my feet, revealing a deep crevasse into nothing. The icy chasm gleamed a deep, dark blue.

I stepped back, my breath short.

"You will walk across that," Varemar said.

It was easily twenty feet across. There was no bridge. I'd have to conjure one.

"No magic," Varemar said.

"What?" Ares barked.

"No magic. It's a test of worthiness."

I held out a hand, cutting off Ares's next words. "So you're suggesting that I walk across thin air on nothing but my own worthiness?"

"Precisely." Varemar's voice was cold.

It was a good thing I couldn't see her expression through her ethereal form. I didn't think I'd like it.

Ares caught my eye. "Don't do it."

I could read the message he didn't say. *We'd find another way.*

But we wouldn't. Couldn't he feel the magic here? This was the land of the primordial ice gods. Without their permission, there was no other way through.

I shot him a brief look, hoping it gave him faith, then turned to the primordial gods. "All I have to do is walk across, right? No magic. Just step onto nothing?"

The three nodded.

I rubbed my hands together. "All right, then. Let's do it."

From behind, I could feel my friends' dismay.

I didn't share it.

Yes, I could go plunging down a thousand foot crevasse. But I wouldn't.

I was the one who would defeat Drakon. This was my purpose. The reason I'd been born. No matter what it took—I would be victorious. I *would* save the world. Because I wouldn't settle for anything less. I was the hero of the gods, chosen by fate, and christened by the Valkyrie and Athena.

Watch out, Hercules.

CHAPTER NINE

My head went completely silent as I stepped off the ledge, straight into thin air. My heart lodged in my throat, but my mind was calm.

I was worthy. I would pass this test.

My foot landed on solid ice. A narrow pillar had shot up from the crevice below, creating a stepping stone for me. I stepped forward again. Another appeared.

I grinned.

Then strode across, the ice rising to meet my every step.

Isedor grumbled, his icy face scowling. He clearly didn't want me to succeed.

Tough cookies, ice grump. I stepped onto the ledge on the other side.

Varemar inclined her head. "You have passed, Phoenix Knight."

"That does not mean that you will succeed," Isedor grumbled. "Or even reach the mountain of dragons."

Ain't that the truth. I also wouldn't necessarily survive the encounter with Drakon. But I *was* worthy of trying.

I turned toward my friends. The crevasse was gone. They stared at me, each of their faces stark white.

Yeah, they weren't pleased I'd taken the risk. But I'd had to. I turned back to the ice giants.

"Can we leave here now?" I asked.

"Yes. Should you need to return, do not come to our door again. You are worthy, thus you and your allies may transport at will onto Svalbard." A swirl of snow drifted off Varemar's ephemeral arm as she pointed to the guards who had led us here. "The Icevar will lead you out."

The gray-cloaked figures moved away from the side wall. Half a dozen of them moved toward the far wall.

"Thank you." I didn't know what else to say to the reluctant gods, so I left it at that and joined the Icevar. My friends followed. Tension thrummed in the air as we walked.

Cass joined me and whispered, "That was iffy."

"No kidding." I glanced back, disconcerted to see the gods all still watching us. Isedor had a particularly dark gleam in his icy eyes. I shivered and turned toward the shadow ones. "Can we go?"

They stalked away, so we followed, walking toward the large doors on the back wall. They swung open of their own volition, revealing an icy courtyard at the back of the castle. Shadows lurked in the corners, a precursor to the threat we'd face outside these walls.

Ares stepped up beside me, his eyes searching for danger.

Wind bit at my cheeks as we stepped outside. The Icevar led us through the wide open courtyard to a large gate. Slowly, it creaked open, revealing a narrow passage bordered on two sides by towering walls of ice. They stretched so far up into the dark sky that I couldn't see the top.

"Oh, shit," Del muttered.

"No kidding." I shuddered, my claustrophobia kicking into high gear.

The Icevar stepped out into the chasm. I followed, Ares behind me, with Del and Cass behind him. I glanced over my shoulder. Bree and Ana were last, with everyone else in the middle.

An ominous weight settled on the air as we followed the Icevar through the chasm. The ice walls loomed high on either side. I swallowed hard, tension tightening my muscles.

"I feel trapped," Cass muttered from behind me.

"Ditto."

The Icevar stalked along, leading us through the dark night. I wished we'd go faster—put more distance between us and the primordial gods. Just the memory of them gave me the willies.

When thundering footsteps sounded from behind us, my heart leapt into my throat.

I spun, peering back into the blackness. Everyone else did the same. The footsteps pounded closer.

"Giant," Ares said.

He was right. That was the only thing that could have such pounding footsteps. The ground shook with every footfall, chips of ice raining down from the walls.

If one of the gods had changed their minds about letting us pass, we couldn't fight them. My skin chilled.

"Run!" I cried.

Right before I turned, I caught sight of Isedor, his icy, angular form hurtling through the chasm, straight at us.

Oh shit. He'd been the meanest one.

I sprinted across the ice, suddenly realizing that the Icevar had disappeared. When the first massive bolt of ice plowed into the ground in front of me, I realized why.

They didn't want to be caught by Isedor's weapons.

I raced, my lungs burning. My friends' footsteps pounded behind me as we sprinted away from the immortal ice giant. Icicles slammed into the ground all around us. I kept glancing back, trying to get a feel for where they might land. I ducked and dodged, along with my friends.

We didn't really have the power to fight a primordial god who was also a giant. But he was gaining on us.

Running wasn't working.

He was only fifty yards away now.

Something hard and heavy slammed into my arm. I crashed to the ground as a massive icicle plowed into the ice next to me. Pain surged through my arm as I scrambled up.

Mordaca was down, too, but climbing to her feet.

At least we weren't bleeding, but the blunt force had rocked me. But there was no time to recover.

We had to fight.

I turned toward the giant. Bree and Ana, who'd been last in line, had turned to face him as well. They were closest, the two youngest of us right in his line of fire.

Ana threw out her hands, conjuring one of her magical shields. It blazed blue and bright, a dome of light. The magic slammed into my chest.

Damn, that girl was strong. Stronger than I'd realized.

Isedor roared, throwing a large icicle at her shield. It crashed into the blue magic, shattering on impact. Ana stumbled backward, clearly feeling the blow. Isedor threw another icicle, and it collided with her shield.

She went to her knees, but her magical shield stayed strong.

Bree, who was several meters behind Ana, sprinted toward her and Isedor. She slid under the magical shield, then leapt to her feet and hurled a blast of magic at the giant.

The sonic boom exploded, blasting into his chest and throwing him backward. It was so strong that shards of ice flew off him. He was breaking apart! Around him, the ice walls shattered, huge chunks tumbling down on him.

Just then, the magic ricocheted back at us, destroying Ana's shield and throwing me to the ground. I slammed into the ice, dazed at the sheer power of her blow.

Sonic booms didn't travel *backward*.

But apparently Bree's did.

I gasped, trying to drag air into my aching lungs. All around me, my friends were flat on their backs.

Bree had magic the likes of which I'd never seen.

After a few gasping minutes, I managed to climb to my feet. Every part of me ached.

"Everyone okay?" The words were torture to get out.

A chorus of groans and yeses sounded as everyone slowly climbed to their feet. I staggered toward Bree and Ana, who were both still on the ground. In front of them, a huge pile of ice buried Isedor.

Awe filled me. I didn't know what Bree and Ana were, but it was something *powerful*.

I fell to my knees at Ana's side. She lay flat on her back, blinking at the sky. Her pale hair fanned out against the ice. It was longer than it had been. Her skin was nearly white, her blue eyes stark in her face.

"You okay?" I asked.

She coughed, a bit of blood trickling from the corner of her mouth. Panic spiked.

"Ana!" I touched her shoulder.

"Fine." She gasped, curling over in pain. "Normal. Check Bree."

"You mean this is normal? To be coughing blood after using your magic."

She grimaced. "This much, yeah. Bree."

I scrambled around to find Bree.

Ares knelt at her side. He looked up. "Passed out cold."

Shit. I turned back to Ana. "Will she be okay? Will you?"

She nodded, the motion clearly painful. "Tapped out."

"No wonder. You defeated a god."

A smile tugged at the corner of her mouth, then she winced. "Shouldn't use that much. No control."

That much magic? I opened my mouth to ask, but her eyes rolled back into her head and she passed out.

I looked up. My friends stood around, arms wrapped around aching ribs and faces twisted into grimaces. "Bree and Ana are out. Can you take them back, Mordaca? Get them to a healer."

Mordaca nodded, stepping forward. She limped slightly. "Will I be able to find you again if I return?"

"I think so," I said. "The gods said that now that we've gained entry, we don't have to pass their way again. Can you transport back to Aerdeca?"

"I can." She knelt between Bree and Ana, then touched their arms. She looked at the rest of us. "See you in a bit."

A moment later, the three of them disappeared.

I stood, my whole body aching.

"Badass." Del's voice was strained with pain.

"Yeah, those girls mean business." Cass winced.

"What are they?" Claire asked.

I shrugged, then regretted the action when pain raced through me. "No idea. They hide it."

"And that magic." Ares whistled.

"It knocked them out pretty hard," I said. "They need more control."

"But how do you practice something like that?" Connor asked. "The Order would want to know about Magica that strong and uncontrolled. I'm not sure they'd like it."

No, they probably wouldn't. Anyone who could take out a god was a potential threat, especially if they couldn't reliably control their magic. It was one reason the Order didn't like FireSouls. Not only could we steal magic, but that gave us strength that frightened them. The world relied on balance. Girls with power like Ana's and Bree's—or ours—threatened that balance.

"Well, we won't speak of it," Claire said. "That's their business."

"Good plan." I nodded toward the chasm. "Let's keep moving."

I stepped forward, my whole body singing with pain. I gasped and clutched at my ribs. Everything hurt from the blast that had thrown us to the ground. Sonic booms—really strong ones—could pulverize bones and organs as well as hurl you backward.

Everyone else looked like they felt like hell too. Standing around and talking had been hard enough. But moving after a sonic boom with that power? No way. Hell, we'd only gotten a bit of the blowback.

"I've got something to help." Connor dug into his potion bag, movement slow and face pained. He pulled out two vials and passed them around. "A sip each should do it. We need to ration."

Cass drank first. Immediately, her features smoothed. The pain must have faded. She passed it to me. I took a tiny sip of the sickly sweet liquid and nearly gagged. But the relief that flowed through my body made me sag with pleasure.

"Amazing." I passed the vial to Ares.

Within moments, we were all stronger. Nearly back to normal. The vials were only half empty, too, which was a real win.

Aerdeca and Roarke handed them back to Connor, who tucked them into his bag.

"Thanks," I said.

He grinned. "Anytime."

I turned toward the chasm exit and started forward. It was a cold, dark trek. We jogged, trying to put as much space as possible between us and the primordial god. Tension thickened the air as we waited for Isedor to climb out of the ice rubble and come after us, but he never did. All the same, sweat rolled down my spine.

When we finally spilled out onto a massive plane of snow, the aurora borealis had filled the night sky. It gleamed green and yellow as the fabulous light roiled across the sky, illuminating the field of snow below.

Ares stopped next to me. "Where to?"

I called upon my dragon sense, letting it tug around my middle and direct me. I pointed ahead and to the left. "That way."

"Oh yeah," Del murmured. "Dragons thataway."

I looked at her. "You feel it?"

"Like a homing beacon." Cass rubbed her hands together. "Let's get a move on."

We set off across the icy snow, wind whipping across our cheeks. Mordaca joined us after about twenty minutes.

I caught her eye. "Bree and Ana okay?"

"Still unconscious but alive. The healer is with them."

"Thanks. You okay?"

"Yeah. He gave me a pick-me-up potion."

"Good." I turned back and started forward again.

We hiked in silence, the aurora borealis drifting across the sky. When the ground began to tremble beneath us, I stiffened.

Isedor?

I turned.

"What's coming?" Claire drew her sword.

I squinted into the dark, my breath caught.

When the icy figures thundered over the horizon, my mind blanked.

"Not Isedor," Cass said.

"But what *are* they?" They looked like giant dogs made of ice, but when I spotted a pair of huge tusks, I gasped. "Woolly mammoths!"

"Made of ice." Cass's magic swelled as she gathered it to her. "We can't outrun them."

Del nodded. "Anything on four legs is faster than those on two."

There were at least six mammoths running across the snow toward us. Their icy bodies glittered in the light.

"Damn, the dragons picked a good place to hide," I muttered.

"It's protected, at least." Ares drew his shadow sword. It could cut through anything, but how many cuts would it need to take down a giant mammoth? You could strike the heart of a flesh and blood mammoth—but what stopped an ice beast?

"I can create a barrier," Del said.

I nodded at her, then shouted to everyone else, "Form a line!"

We took up positions, standing in a row, ready to face the mammoths. Del used her gift over ice and snow to create three icy walls in front of us. They each stood at least eight feet tall and three feet thick.

"Hopefully that'll slow them," she said.

"I hope so." I conjured my bow and arrows. I'd make them flame.

Cass leapt onto the top of the wall that blocked us. I joined her, Connor and Claire at my side. Everyone else jumped up too.

When the mammoths were close enough to hit, Cass conjured a massive fireball and hurled it at one of the mammoths. It exploded against his chest. The beast stumbled, but quickly righted itself, stampeding toward our first ice wall. Five others ran at his side.

Claire, a fire mage, conjured another fireball. She hurled it at the same mammoth. This time, he went to his knees, but still managed to right himself.

"Not good!" Claire shouted.

"Nope!" Cass threw another blast of flame.

I took up position next to Aerdeca, who also used a bow, and conjured a bucket of flaming oil and a pile of arrows wrapped with rags. I looked at her. "Use these."

She nodded and grabbed an arrow, igniting it in the oil and then firing at the nearest mammoth. I joined her, releasing my arrows in quick succession. They plunged into the mammoth's icy hides, flames flickering, but didn't slow the beasts.

My heart pounded as they neared us, impervious to our weapons. Primordial magic sure was a witch to defeat.

The two mammoths in the lead plowed through Del's first ice wall. Snow and chips of ice exploded outward. The wall slowed them, but barely. They were now only fifty feet away.

"We're not doing so hot," Aerdeca muttered.

If I hadn't been so scared, I would have laughed at her wry tone.

Connor chucked an acid green potion bomb that burst against the chest of an oncoming mammoth. The beast thundered forward, silent as the acid ate away at his icy chest.

It made me feel better that these magic beasts didn't feel pain. I mean, they'd probably stomp us to death, but still ... Made me feel better.

Ares leapt off the wall and sprinted toward the oncoming mammoths.

My heart jumped into my throat. "Ares!"

He didn't turn, just raced for a mammoth that was headed for the second ice wall. He scaled the wall, reached the top, then leapt onto the mammoth's back. The beast bucked, rising up on two sturdy back legs, but Ares clung tightly.

When the mammoth's front feet slammed back onto the ground, Ares raised his shadow sword high and plunged it into the back of the mammoth's neck. The beast shuddered, then collapsed. Ares rolled off.

"Yes!" I fired an arrow, victory singing through me. My arrows might only slow the mammoths, but Ares could take them out.

But then the mammoth lumbered to its feet. It backed up, clearly intending to plow through the second ice wall.

"Well, shit," Aerdeca muttered.

"There's no killing these magic beasts!" Cass fired another massive fireball.

It stunned an oncoming mammoth temporarily, but the creature eventually continued forward. It crashed through the ice wall, along with the mammoth that Ares had temporarily felled. Four of its brethren followed behind, pounding toward us across the snow.

My heartbeat thundered in my ears. We were staring down death by stomping and it sucked.

They were only about thirty feet away by now. We stood on the last ice wall. We'd have to retreat.

Damn, we needed help. Some major firepower to defeat these ice beasts.

Jeff! And the Pūķi.

I called to them with my mind, having no idea if it'd work. It'd seemed to in the past, however unconsciously.

A moment later, the three dragons appeared. Jeff took quick stock of the situation, his alert onyx gaze darting around. Fortunately, he was in his large form again. As big as a car. He plunged toward the nearest ice mammoth and shot a blast of flame at the creature. The mammoth reared up on its hind legs, shying away from the fire.

Though we hadn't managed to disable him with our paltry flames, Jeff was holding him off. The Pūķi followed suit, charging for the others.

"Run!" I cried.

We scrambled down from the ice wall and sprinted across the snow. My lungs burned as I ran, desperate to leave the mammoths behind.

"I'd kill for a ride," Del panted.

Seconded. I couldn't speak the words aloud, however. Too out of breath.

A moment later, thirteen massive dogs appeared around us. Briefly, my heart jumped into my throat. Then I recognized them.

I gasped at Del. "Your hellhounds!" I slowed to a jog.

"Pond Flower!" she cried.

The brown and white spotted hellhound charged for her. Pond Flower had named herself, according to Del, who had a connection with the animals and could understand them. Pond Flower looked like a massive hound dog, except for the eyes of flame and the occasional black fire that rose up from her gleaming coat.

Pond Flower barked excitedly. Her compatriots joined in.

"They want to pull us!" Del said. "Like sled dogs."

I grinned, relief surging through me. "All right."

We slowed to a halt. I glanced behind to make sure the mammoths were held off. Jeff and the Pūki were doing a good job, but there were more mammoths than dragons. It was all my allies could do just to slow them. They were about a hundred yards off now, but slowly gaining.

We needed to be quick.

I turned back to the hellhounds. There were thirteen of them and ten of us. I conjured three big sleds and harnesses, hoping that the dogs were strong enough.

Quickly, we hitched the dogs to the sleds. I had to make some adjustments to my conjured harnesses, but we were ready to go within minutes.

Pond Flower barked from the front of her sled. Like Rudolph, with her flaming eyes so bright, she led four other dogs.

I pointed to her sled. "Aerdeca, Mordaca, Connor, and Claire."

They climbed into the sled. As soon as they were settled, the dogs took off, shooting across the snow.

Ares whistled. "Not bad."

"No kidding." I glanced behind me. The mammoths were now fifty yards away, the dragons darting around them, blasting flames to slow their progress. "Let's get in."

Ares and I joined Del in one of the sleds, while Cass, Aidan, and Roarke got on another. I sat in the middle, between Del in the front and Ares in the back. Our dogs took off right away. They sped through the snow, their unnatural strength zipping us along. Wind tore at my hair, and the aurora borealis shined down on the hellhounds who plowed across the snow.

I looked back. We were leaving the mammoths in the dust. The dragons darted around them, blasting flames.

I almost laughed. My life was freaking scary a lot of the time, but there were perks. Like hellhound sleigh rides beneath a magical sky while dragons protected us from ice mammoths. I saw a lot of fabulous things, but this topped most of them.

The dogs pulled us across the snow, moving faster than any normal dog ever could. Within an hour, mountain peaks began to appear on the horizon. Magic thrummed on the air.

"Feel that?" Del shouted.

"Yeah!" I shuddered. It was dark magic. Drakon's, not the dragons.

As we neared, it became possible to see the mist surrounding the top of the tallest mountain. The aurora borealis made it glow green, an eerie sight.

"That's their mountain," Ares said.

"Yeah." Another thrum of magic, this one feeling like home, vibrated in my chest. It was coming from the left, in the mountain. Particularly strong in one area.

There were dragons in there. *Real* dragons.

I leaned around to speak in Del's ear. "Sense that?"

She nodded. "Dragons."

"So weird." And amazing.

One of the hellhounds barked, excitement palpable in the sound. I glanced sharply toward it. We didn't need any more noise. In front of me, Del swiped her hand through the air, her magic swelling. The sounds dampened.

I rubbed her arm in thanks.

We rode silently through the snow, the dark magic rolling over us. Drakon and his army were definitely here. We needed shelter. A place to hide while we plotted our next step.

I pointed toward a rock outcropping at the base of the mountain. The black rocks jutted toward the sky. "Ask the dogs to take us there."

Del nodded. The dogs diverted their course and headed straight for the rocks. They pulled to a stop, and we all clambered off.

"Thank you," I said to the dogs.

A few moments later, they disappeared.

"Are our sounds still dampened?" I whispered.

Del nodded. "We can hear each other, but our voices shouldn't travel far."

"Thanks." I was damned glad she'd taken this power from a miserable demon.

We all huddled in the shelter of the dark rocks. Drakon's dark magic seethed in the air. It was stronger now—either because of him or because he had a massive demon army.

"We have to scout the terrain," Ares said.

"Agreed." I looked toward Cass and Aidan. "Can you two pull your bird trick?"

"Sure thing." Cass grinned.

"I wish I could see too." Cass would transform into a bird and scout the terrain, and no doubt she'd do a good job, but I wanted to see firsthand.

"I can help with that," Aerdeca said.

My gaze darted to her. "Yeah?"

She nodded. "Hold out your wrist. Both of you. I can give you Cass's vision."

I stuck out my wrist, yanking up my sleeve to reveal my pale skin. Cass did the same. Aerdeca withdrew a small silver knife from her pocket, then made a small incision on my wrist. Pain flared and blood welled. She did the same to Cass, then gripped our wrists and pressed our wounds together.

"Good thing I like you," I murmured to Cass.

She chuckled.

Aerdeca began to recite some strange words in a language I'd never heard. The world spun around me, white and black with flashes of green aurora borealis. Then my muscles sagged and my vision changed.

Suddenly I was looking at *myself.*

I must be in Cass's eyes.

Damn, I needed a shower. I looked rough. Had I looked like this ever since Drakon had showed up on the scene? Yeah, probably.

"It worked." My stomach turned. It was nauseating to see from another person's perspective, like my body knew this was seriously off.

"Good." Aerdeca dropped our wrists. "It should last about twenty minutes, so get a move on."

The world bobbled in front of my eyes, and I had to assume that Cass was nodding her head. I reached out a hand. "Ares?"

He gripped mine, pulling me against him. I leaned into him. I felt blind, but not. Though I could see, the world that filtered into my brain had nothing to do with where I was or what I was actually doing. It was all Cass.

Golden magic swirled in front of my eyes. *She must be shifting into a sparrow.*

Then the world changed. Everyone around me loomed high above, even myself.

"She's a sparrow now," Ares said. "Sitting on the ground."

My vision turned left. I saw another sparrow. *Must be Aidan.*

He launched himself into the air. Cass must have followed, because suddenly the world zipped by in front of me. My friends disappeared, and soon I saw the ground from above, a massive expanse of white stretching as far as the eye could see.

In the shadows of the dark rocks, I could just barely make out the specks that were my friends. And me. We were pretty well camouflaged, actually.

Cass whirled on the air, flying away toward the misty mountain. It shimmered through the mist that glinted green. As she flew, the landscape whipped by beneath her.

I swore I could feel the wind in my feathers, the cool breeze on my sparrow face.

When the army appeared in the snow, I almost screamed. I'd become so relaxed and enchanted by the surreal flight that I'd drifted into a semi-dream state.

But there were hundreds of them, demons camped out in the valley beyond. Cass kept high above them, no doubt wanting to avoid detection. It was still easy to see how many there were, though.

Too damned many.

At least two hundred. All different species from all over. There could be some dragon tattoo gang members down there, too, but it didn't matter even if there were. We'd dispatched a lot of them, but there were always more who were willing to side with evil.

Cass flew, her gaze sweeping over the entirety of the valley below.

She was searching for Drakon.

But he was nowhere to be found.

An explosion rocked the night air, a sound so loud that my head rang with noise. It blasted me onto my side. Snow scraped against my cheek. Panic raced through me.

The dragons!

CHAPTER TEN

I scrambled upright, hands dug into the snow for purchase. All around me, my friends rose woozily.

I could see again, through my own eyes. It hadn't been twenty minutes, but maybe the explosion had knocked me out of Cass's vision.

Horror opened in my chest.

I gasped, searching the sky above. "Cass!"

Had something happened to her?

The dragons' mountain that we were crouched beneath was belching black smoke. The whole top was blown off. I ignored it as my heart pounded, searching the sky for two sparrows.

"I don't see them." Panic thrummed in Del's voice.

Had they been caught in the explosion? Was that why I was no longer in her sight?

We all searched the sky, our fear palpable on the air. I could almost smell it. I gripped Ares's hand hard as worry choked me.

Finally, through the dark bellowing smoke, two tiny sparrows hurtled toward us. They slowed their frantic descent at the last minute, tumbling in the snow.

Magic gleamed gold around them as they shifted back to human form.

I lunged for Cass, hugging her. "I thought you were caught in the blast!"

"So did I." She squeezed me and pulled back, her eyes wide. "Did you see them all?"

"All what?" Ares demanded.

I turned to him. "Demons. He has an army of hundreds."

"Shit." Ares dragged a hand over his face.

Roarke's gaze turned dark. Del squeezed his shoulder.

"My fault," Roarke gritted.

"You were helping us," I said. "That kept you out of the Underworld."

"All the same." He scowled.

"All the same what?" Del demanded. "You don't control all the realms and all the portals. It's impossible. Don't blame yourself. Just get to helping now."

He gave her a long look, one of appreciation and respect. They balanced each other well. And Del was right. He was Warden of the Underworld, not a god.

"So there are hundreds of demons and not hundreds of us," I said. "And I'm not even sure we can raise an army to defeat that many."

"We've got allies," Del said.

"The Vampire Court and our soldiers will help," Ares said.

"There's others, too," Cass said. "Maybe the shifters and the Order."

"If they're willing. Even then, it may not be enough." I watched the smoke billowing overhead. Drakon was going straight for the dragons. He didn't have his tools yet—he still needed one of us—but he was preparing. The idea of him harming the dragons while they slept made my stomach turn. "Drakon is ready for us. And he doesn't even realize that we probably can't fight his whole army."

"Only one thing can defeat Drakon," Ares said.

Understanding dawned on me. Of course. We couldn't fight the dragons' battle. Only they could. "We have to wake the dragons."

"Wake them?" Aerdeca gasped. "Are you serious?"

"How will they know we're not the enemy?" Mordaca asked.

I shrugged. "Maybe they won't. But if we can't fight Drakon and guarantee a win, they need a chance to defend themselves."

"Or they'll die in their sleep." Horror painted Del's face. Everyone's, actually.

"We'll still fight for them," I said. "But they need a chance to fight for themselves."

"How do we wake dragons?" Claire asked.

"No idea." I stared at the mountain, letting the varying magical signatures rush over me. There was Drakon's, which felt like tar coating my organs, but then there was that wonderful feeling of home that'd I'd felt earlier. "Can anyone else feel the good magic?"

"Good magic?" Connor asked.

"Yeah. Something that feels like home. Not like Drakon's garbage signature."

"I can," Cass said. "Feels like being in my trove."

"Same," Del said.

"Only the FireSouls feel it, then," Ares said.

"I think it's the dragons." I nodded, convinced. "Has to be."

"I think we need to follow it," Del said. "We need a way to reach them, and we can't go Drakon's way."

"Yeah, I'm not keen on tangling with him right now," Cass said.

"Or his army," Connor added.

"I think there's another way. We just need to follow the magic." I turned, trying to get a feel for which way it pulled me. "Follow me."

I led the way, Cass and Del at my side. When I lost the signal, one of them picked it up. Together, we climbed up the steep side of the mountain. Fortunately, the aurora borealis had faded, plunging the night into darkness. I still felt like a sitting duck out here on the slope, but I'd take whatever cover I could get.

"It's growing stronger," Cass said.

"Definitely close," Del added.

The mountain still loomed high overhead. We'd only gone about a third of the way up, but Del was definitely right. The entrance was near.

To the left, a vertical outcropping caught my eye. It was covered in ice. I turned toward it, skidding on the slope. When I stopped in front of it, Ares raised a glowing hand and shed some light on the surface. The ice was at least two inches thick, covering black rock that looked inscribed.

"Can you melt this?" I asked Claire.

Claire stepped forward, fire blazing from her palm. It took only a minute and the ice melted away. We all huddled around the stone, trying to read the strange inscriptions.

I could almost make them out, like it was a language I'd once studied in school but long since forgotten.

But I'd never studied this language. These characters weren't anything I'd seen before.

"It's a dead language," Aerdeca said.

"But I think I recognize it," Cass said.

I looked at her. "You too?"

"And me," Del said.

"No coincidence there, then," Connor said.

We studied the stone. Soon, the letters began to make sense. Sort of.

"I think we have to give it something," Del said.

As soon as she said it, the words clicked into place. "Our blood. We have to smear some FireSoul blood on it to gain entrance."

"Easy enough." Cass pulled one of her trusty daggers from the sheath at her thigh and sliced the fleshy part of her palm. She handed the dagger off to me, then pressed her wound against the stone.

Del and I followed suit. Pain flared as I sliced my hand. As soon as we'd all touched the black stone, magic swirled around us. The stone glowed a pale white, then disappeared.

A long tunnel stretched into darkness.

"Whoa." Del grinned.

"Yeah." I turned to my friends. "Straight to dragons."

Claire edged up beside us. "You guys know how to party."

"Walking into scary black tunnels in search of dragons?" I asked. "Heck yeah, we do."

"Let's get some light." Claire held out her palms. Glowing balls of fire formed, then floated off into the air, drifting down the tunnel.

I whistled. "Nice."

"Been practicing."

I stepped into the tunnel. Magic sparked on the air, that familiar feeling of home. As if the dragons were welcoming us.

"Keep a wary eye out," Ares said.

"You still can't feel the magic?" I asked.

"No."

"If there's a threat, it's not coming from the tunnel or the dragons." I certainly wasn't relaxed—but this tunnel didn't frighten me. "This place wants us here. Drakon, on the other hand...."

Ares grunted, clearly still concerned.

We set off down the passage, which was wide enough to allow us to walk three abreast. Claire's glowing fire floated along in front of us, illuminating our passage. The walls around us gleamed black and shiny. Obsidian, I realized.

As we walked, the magic grew stronger and the heat higher.

"I sure hope there's not lava in here," I muttered. I'd had enough with the vampire trials.

It took us twenty minutes of silent walking to reach the massive cavern within. When the tunnel opened up to the mountain's core, I hesitated at the tunnel exit, awe filling me.

The space within was massive, a hollowed mountain. A great pit in the middle emitted a glowing white light. It was surrounded by a wide ledge all around.

Three dragons slept on the ledge, each in their own little section, separate from the others. They were massive—one hundred feet long, at least. They slept, curled up like cats, but that was where the resemblance ended.

Even though I was here to save them—and they in turn could save us—they were still really freaking scary. Their scales glinted in the light. One was a gleaming black, one a shining silver, and the last a pearly white. Their heads were enormous, with large fangs protruding from their mouths. Spikes decorated their spines, and their huge wings were folded around their bodies like blankets. Claws as long as a person tipped their front and back feet.

And their magic—that smacked me in the face like a hit of pure power. It was both welcoming and terrifying.

These guys were *definitely* the source of all magic. I'd known it before—but that had been intellectually. This … This was a knowing deep in my gut.

"Wow."

I wasn't sure who said it, probably everyone, actually. Even me. I'd never been so awed in my life.

"They're real," Connor murmured.

"Sure are." I studied the nearest one—the silver. He had flecks of blue on his scales, pale and shiny. His nostrils quivered as he slept.

I inspected the rest of the cavern, searching for threats. Above us, the mountain opened to the sky. Drakon had blown the peak right off, but it was three thousand feet to the top, maybe more. I saw no movement at the top or on the walls.

They hadn't ventured down yet. Would they? Or would they perform their dark magic from the rim?

If I were them, I'd stay the hell away from the dragons.

"I feel no demon magic," Cass whispered.

"Neither do I," Del said.

"It's clear." Ares looked around. "For now."

"Then we'd better hurry." I stepped forward, then turned back to my friends. "We'll start with Cass, Del, and me trying to wake them. If they're dangerous, they're less likely to hurt us. Can the rest of you keep guard?"

There was a chorus of ayes, and I turned, walking toward the pit in the middle. It was at least a hundred yards across, and I wanted to know what the heck was down there. It wasn't hot enough to be lava, though the steamy light that rose from it was warm.

I edged toward the lip, then peered over. Bright light shined far below, like the core of the earth was made of a shining diamond. I couldn't see the bottom. Just light.

"Any idea what's down there?" I asked Del and Cass, who were at my side.

"Not a clue," Del said.

"Feels like magic," Cass added. "Not sure what kind."

I focused on it, trying to get a feel for the signature. It felt vaguely like a breath of fresh, life-giving air. And smelled of green grass. Tasted of a good meal, though I couldn't for the life of me determine what exactly.

"I think it's life. Like my magic. Kinda." I turned toward the nearest dragon. The silver one. The white light from the pit shined up toward the hole at the top of the mountain, but it also drifted toward the dragon, encapsulating him in its glow. "I think the magic is helping the dragons. Keeping them alive or something."

"I see that," Cass said. "And feel it."

I walked toward the silver dragon, going right up to his head.

Intense awareness heightened my senses. Up close, I could see movement behind his eyelids, as if he were dreaming. The magic was even stronger near him, and his scales were even more beautiful up close.

"I can hardly breathe, this is so exciting," Del whispered.

"No kidding." With my *deirfiúr* at my side, I reached out and touched the dragon's neck. His scales were smooth beneath my hand, and a dull noise roared in my head.

A *dragon*. A real, freaking dragon.

He didn't shift at my touch, so I stroked him and murmured, "Time to wake up."

He didn't move an inch. I glanced at Del and Cass, unsure.

How exactly did one wake a dragon?

"Rise and shine!" Cass said in a cheerful voice.

I almost choked on horrified laughter. But the dragon just snuffled and shifted.

I rubbed him a bit harder, trying to give him a shake. But he was so big he didn't budge. We each pressed our hands to his side, talking to him. Murmuring gibberish about waking up and saving themselves and the world.

The dragon lay still.

I turned toward Connor, who stood at the tunnel exit with everyone else. "Can I have the rest of that healing potion?"

It'd given me a great burst of energy, so maybe it'd work on the dragon.

Connor nodded and stepped forward, digging into his bag as he approached. He handed me one of the vials, and I uncorked it, then walked around to the dragon's mouth.

"Ooh, boy. Big teeth." My gaze riveted to them, unable to look away. I was here to help the dragon—I just hope he realized that when he woke. Because one chomp….

I wedged the vial between the dragon's lips, then tilted. The liquid poured out, disappearing.

We all waited, breath held. The only sound in the room was the subtle whooshing of air from the dragon's nostrils.

But the beast didn't stir.

"Damn." I frowned.

"We can try noise," Del said. "I'll create a sound barrier above. Then we'll make noise down here."

"I can make an exploding sound," Connor said.

I nodded. "Let's try it."

Del sucked in a deep breath, and her magic swelled, bringing with it the scent of clean soap and the feel of soft grass beneath my feet. Eventually, she nodded. "We're good."

Connor walked away from the dragons, about fifty yards, then pulled a potion bomb from his pack. "Everyone, cover your ears!"

I did as he said. Then he hurled the potion bomb to the ground. It shattered on the stone, and white dust billowed up, followed by a loud boom that shook my bones.

The dragons didn't stir.

"Shit."

"We could light a fire under their asses," Claire said. "Literally."

"No way," I said.

"Not enough to burn them! I'd make sure it was far enough away."

"I know, but I don't want to start with anything that could be a threat."

"We can try something," Aerdeca said.

I gestured toward the sleeping dragon. "Have at it."

The sisters approached the dragon, awe on their faces. They stopped in front of his head. I joined them. Mordaca reached into a pocket and withdrew a silver knife. She sliced it over her palm. Black blood welled.

Whoa. That was weird.

Aerdeca did the same. Oddly enough, her blood was a pearly

white. If it even was blood. And it seemed that their color preference didn't extend just to their clothes.

The two sisters joined hands, letting their blood mingle, then began to recite an incantation. Their low voices vibrated with power. Wind—coming from nowhere—blew my hair back from my face. My veins began to sparkle with energy. It flowed through me, making me shiver.

Was this what the dragons felt?

I hoped so.

But nothing happened. The dragon continued to slumber.

"We're going to check out the other one," Cass murmured.

I nodded absently, watching the dragon as the Blood Sorceresses' magic flowed through me, stronger and stronger. They were giving it all they had.

Come on, come on....

Finally, Aerdeca and Mordaca stepped back, their gazes disappointed.

"Not going to work," Aerdeca said.

"That's never happened before." Mordaca huffed. "You've got some stubborn dragons."

"They've been asleep centuries," I said. "According to the Valkyrie, they're low on power. That may be part of it."

"We can try another dragon," Ares said.

"It's our only shot." I turned to find Cass and Del. They'd said they would try another. I spotted them by the black dragon, about one hundred yards away. Roarke and Aidan were with them. They circled the dragon, no doubt looking for a clue.

Please find one.

A scratching noise from above caught my attention. I looked up, searching the black wall that rose toward the mountain's top.

They were *moving.* The rocks weren't rocks at all.

I pointed. "What the hell is that?"

Everyone's gazes went toward the shifting black wall. A few

rocks tumbled down from the side. Tension tightened my muscles.

"Cass! Del! The wall near you is—"

Demons leapt from the wall above, black as obsidian and camouflaged like the stone. They landed with a *thud* between Cass and Del, who stood near the dragon's tail.

"No!" I shrieked, racing for them.

Del drew her sword, but before it was fully out of the ether, one of the stone demons was upon her, wrapping strong arms around her waist. A half second later, she disappeared, transported elsewhere.

Another demon was on Cass a moment later. I was still fifty yards away. She hurled a massive fireball at the demon, which knocked him out. But a millisecond later, a large rock plummeted from above, hitting her on the head.

Time slowed as I ran, watching her get swooped up by a demon and transported away. And Roarke and Aidan were nowhere to be found. Had they already been abducted?

"No!" I sprinted for them, as if I could find them even though they'd disappeared.

A hard arm wrapped around my waist, dragging me to a stop. A second later, the ether sucked me in.

I gasped, stumbling.

My vision cleared, revealing the interior of Potions & Pastilles.

Ares stood next to me.

"What did you do?" I shrieked.

He was gone a moment later. Mordaca appeared then, Aerdeca and Claire with her. I stared, stunned. A second later, Ares appeared with Connor.

"The rest are gone," he said. "Abducted."

"I know that!" I shrieked. I sounded crazed to my own ears. "We have to rescue them!"

"We can't do that while trapped," Ares said. "They were gone, and more demons were coming."

"Live to fight another day." Mordaca gripped my shoulders and shook, her dark eyes intense. Promising. "We'll get Cass and Del back."

"And Aidan and Roarke," Claire added.

"If they're even still alive!" Fear spiked in my chest, and I began to pace, vibrating with rage and fear. "Drakon has them! Everything we'd tried to avoid is coming true."

"We grew lazy," Ares said.

"The dragons made it feel safe," Claire said. "And we were too distracted by them."

She was right. That *home* feeling that the dragons emitted had influenced me too. I'd felt safe there. Protected. Cass and Del too. We'd let our guard down.

I shook my head, tears smarting my eyes. "I've never seen demons so well camouflaged."

"I didn't even know they existed," Claire said. "Not truly. Not more than myth."

Connor sagged into a wooden chair, resting his hands on his head.

Claire leaned over him. "Are you all right?"

"Bit woozy is all." He smiled weakly at her. "Fine though."

Now that he said it, I felt it too. In fact, everyone looked like they were swaying on their feet.

"We're exhausted," Aerdeca said. "Not beaten in spirit, but we need to rest a short while. Gain our strength. Then we get more allies, and we go for Cass and Del."

"We can't wait." I started to pace again, but my muscles trembled, weak as noodles.

"The dragon's magic has affected us," Ares said. "Along with our trek. And Aerdeca is right, we need allies when we go back."

"We can't wait!" Panic welled in my chest. I'd lost Del and Cass. They were in Drakon's hands. I couldn't leave them there!

"It has to wait." Ares gripped my arms, his touch grounding. Comforting. "Just a few hours to regain our strength and increase our numbers. And remember—it takes time for Drakon's spell to work. It took days—probably would have taken weeks—to steal the magic from your town. It'll take longer to steal the magic from the dragons."

"Much longer," Mordaca said. "That's probably why the army is there. To defend the spell while it works."

"That means we have time," Ares said. "We'll rest a short while, gather allies, and make a plan. It was impossible to wake the dragons, so we'll have to fight."

"It'll be a death sentence," I said. "You saw the size of that army."

"Then we just need more fighters. And they need to be stronger."

I nodded, swallowing hard. He was right. We just had to be smart. Prepared. "All right. We'll each try to muster troops. Roarke and Aidan made inroads with the Order of the Magica and the Shifter Council. We can use their names when we contact them. Tell them that they've been abducted. I'll see what I can do with the League of FireSouls and my mother's people. The rest of you…gather who you can. And rest. We'll leave in ten hours."

CHAPTER ELEVEN

It didn't take me long to contact the FireSouls or my mother. Both agreed to meet at Factory Row in ten hours, ready for battle. They'd bring everyone they could muster, and we'd all go through a portal to Svalbard.

Fortunately, Mordaca had proven that we could return via transporting once we'd been permitted access by the primordial gods. Hopefully a portal would be allowed as well.

Ares was still in the Vampire Realm, gathering as many troops as he could. Jeff was nowhere to be found, but I wasn't worried. Not about him, at least. He'd show when I called. Claire was trying to find mercenaries from the Order of the Magica to fight, while Aerdeca had gone to the Shifter Council.

Now, it was time to sleep and regain my energy. The fight was coming, and I needed to be ready. But anxiety for Cass and Del clawed at me, raking my insides. Though it was physically painful, I didn't try to ignore it. My negligence had gotten them caught. So I had to be better. I had to use this one chance.

But how?

The question rolled through my mind as I made my way

toward my bed. Though I needed a shower, there was no way I had the energy or the time. Everyone had been right—the dragon's magic had been such a shock to the system that it had weakened us. Added to that, I couldn't remember when I'd slept last.

I fell face-first onto the bed, hoping that a genius plan would come to me in sleep. Something epic and amazing.

If I was still going to save the day, I'd definitely need something along those lines.

∽

The dream slammed into me, short and fast. I was in the dragons' mountain, standing at the edge of the pit. Around me, the dragons slept. At my side, strangely enough, stood the forest spirit from Elesius.

"What are you doing here?" I asked.

"Helping."

"How?" She was just a pale wisp of a thing, a person with hardly any substance at all. Still a ghost, pale and white. There was a bit more substance to her than before, maybe because I'd poured some of my life force into her, but she wasn't a real person.

"The answer is obvious, isn't it?" She pushed her leafy hair back from her face. "You are life. The dragons need life."

"But what does that mean?"

She shrugged a slender shoulder. "I think you know. You must become one with them. Like I will."

Her magic pulsed and she glowed. Then she began to break apart, her form turning to mist that drifted up and swirled on the air, mingling with the light that rose from the pit and sustained the dragons.

Within seconds, she was gone.

∽

I woke with a gasp, heart thundering. It was dark in the room.

My gaze sought the clock.

Four a.m.

Had that been real? No. The forest spirit hadn't died—but she *had* tried to tell me something—I could do this without risking any other lives. I had to try. And I had forty minutes before everyone was meant to show up. If I hurried, I could beat them.

"What is it?" Ares's groggy voice sounded from beside me.

I jumped. In my panic, I hadn't realized he'd snuck into bed with me.

"You're back from the Vampire Realm?" I asked, knowing the question was stupid. But he'd startled me. I wasn't at my best.

He sat up and clicked on a light, scrubbing his hand over his face. "Yes. Thought I'd get some sleep." He looked at the clock. "Not much left of that to be had, though."

"No." I shook my head and climbed out of the bed. He looked so handsome. I couldn't believe this would be the last time I'd see him. Tears smarted my eyes. I leaned down and kissed him hard, then straightened.

A confused grin tugged at his mouth, then he was all business. "I rallied a hundred soldiers. The best in our ranks. Along with some volunteers, plus Doyen and Magisteria."

"We won't need them."

His eyes sharpened. "What do you mean?"

"Exactly what I said." I swallowed hard. "I know how to wake the dragons. But I can do it alone. I must do it alone. And I need you to take me."

"How?"

I couldn't tell him. Not when I was pretty sure it meant my death. Because I needed to give the dragons all of my magic. *All* of it. Could I even survive that?

"There's no time. But I do need to get there. Take me, please." Something frightened thrummed in my chest. Maybe it was the dream, maybe it was fear, but I was manic.

His jaw hardened. "No. Not without the army."

"Scared?" It was a low blow, and I knew it. But panic thundered through my veins, making me low and stupid.

His gaze softened. Of course he wouldn't rise to that bait. Not his style.

"No." He climbed out of bed, his broad chest shirtless, and stood towering over me. He gripped my arms, holding me close. "I won't take you. Not alone."

"Why the hell not?"

"Do you recall when Aethelred the Seer predicted that I would lose what I loved most?"

My extremities tingled. Slowly, I nodded.

"That's you, Nix." His gaze turned fierce. "You are what I love most. I can't lose you."

My heart felt like it cracked in two. The ache was fierce. Tears stung my eyes.

Ares really loved me. I'd believed it before when I'd told him, but somehow—this was worse. It was *so real*. What could we have had, if I didn't have to do what I had to do?

But I wouldn't risk all those people's lives if I could help it. We shouldn't take an army if we didn't need them. No need to waste the life. My fate was sealed either way.

But I couldn't stand here with Ares, dreaming of what might have been. Not when I had to wake the dragons.

I pulled away from him. "I'm getting dressed. If you're not downstairs with me in five minutes when I need to go, I'll find a way to get there myself. Mordaca will take me, for the right price."

He scoffed, as if he didn't believe it. I stiffened my shoulders. He'd have to believe it, because I had to do this.

In the dim bedroom, I didn't look at him as I reached blindly for my clothes. I pulled on a Lil' Bub T-shirt, unable to take any joy in the goofy cat.

Should I go look at my trove one more time?

No. It would be harder to walk away.

I tugged on my boots, keenly aware of Ares's presence as he pulled on his shirt. He hadn't said he would help me, but he wasn't saying no. Not yet.

I left the room, not looking at my apartment as I went to the door. I couldn't look at my life as I left it behind. After slipping on my warm jacket, I took the stairs two at a time, hurrying down to the green door. I called to Jeff and the Pūķi as I went, hoping they'd meet me on the street.

I pushed the door open, stepping out into the cold night air.

Dozens of people surrounded me. I stopped still, shocked. Jeff and the Pūķi sat in the back of the crowd, as I'd expected. But the crowd itself—they shouldn't be here yet.

"You're early," I said. I still had thirty-five minutes before they were supposed to meet.

My mother stepped forward, eyes on mine. "We're going off to battle. Doesn't hurt to be a little early."

"The plan has changed." My voice was stiff. It hurt to look at her, knowing I wouldn't see her again. Like I wanted to memorize her features, every line and curve. My father stood next to her.

To the left, Aerdeca and Mordaca stood, their battle gear on, along with a contingent of folks from Darklane. A motley crew, all dressed in black. Behind them, the League of FireSouls. Not all of them, not yet. But the rest would come, I was sure. Each was dressed in burnished red armor, and their faces were set, hard in the glow of the streetlights. They were ready to fight.

Beyond them stood a dark-haired man whom I hadn't seen in months. Our old friend Emile, the Animus Mage. His rats, Ralph and Rufus, sat on his shoulders. Black and white with their whiskers twitching in the wind. Del's hellhounds stood at his side. Though they normally lived with the League of FireSouls, they'd no doubt been drawn by his ability to speak to animals.

"The Order of the Magica agreed to send fifty of their best mercenaries," Claire said from my side. "Fifty more volunteered to come."

I turned to look at her. She was dressed in her fighting leathers, brown hair pulled back from her face. Connor wasn't with her. "Where's your brother?"

"Late." She grinned.

"Not yet." I looked at them all again, catching sight of an unfamiliar bunch to the right. Their magic smelled like animals. Shifters. "You're all early."

"Why were you trying to sneak out?" my mother asked.

Ares stepped up behind me, his chest warm against my back. I ignored him, my heart breaking.

"I've had a dream. I know how to wake the dragons, but if I can do it alone, I should." I raked my gaze over the crowd, desperate for them not to come. "There's no reason to risk your lives."

"Not when you can do it for us, is that it?" A feminine voice sounded from my left.

I turned. Bree, her dark hair pulled up in a ponytail, shot me a challenging look. Something was different about her, weaker in magic, but she was here all the same, dressed for battle. Next to her, Ana's gaze was hard. She was the same—slightly different, as if the great expulsion of power had weakened her somehow.

"We're coming with you," Ana said. "I didn't get my chance to see the mountain of dragons. And I'm not going back to Death Valley until I do."

I shook my head at her, flabbergasted, then looked at the crowd. "There is no point. Once I wake the dragons, the battle is over. They can defeat the demons."

"Can they?" Claire asked. "Are you sure?"

"Yes. They were huge." The memory flashed in front of my mind's eye. They'd been monstrous, terrifying even in sleep. I had faith in them. But more than that, more than anything—I didn't want all my friends and family to die. There were too many demons, and Drakon was too strong. If I was going to lose my life, it was just salt on the wound that they might lose theirs.

"You're being stubborn, Nix," Ares said.

"And also a bit crazy," Mordaca added.

"I'm not." Was I? Panic still raced through me, the knowledge of what I had to do sending me on my ass—figuratively, at least.

"Without a good plan or a way to get in, you can't guarantee you'll reach the dragons," Ares said.

"I'll have Jeff and the Pūķi. They come when I call."

A fair number of the people in the crowd nodded appraisingly. My dragons could get me through to the sleeping ones below. Then, from there, the dragons would take over.

"We *want* to fight." My mother's voice was firm, lecturing. "It is our choice to risk our lives and defend our magic, *not* yours to protect us. That is not your role, Nix."

I stepped back slightly, shocked. But I *was* the protector. It was what I did, and what I wanted to do now. But this was the harshest tone she'd ever taken with me. And she was right. I was trying to decide for them.

"And alone, you can't guarantee that you can save your *deirfiúr*," Ares said. "I don't know what dream you had or what you need to do, but you'll need help to save them. I know you have faith in the dragons, but hedge your bets."

Save my deirfiúr. He was right. *Both* of them were right. I was being crazy. Stress and fear were getting to me.

"It's the nature of a hero to try to sacrifice themselves," my father said. "To protect others. But Nix—you must accept our help. Because we will come anyway. Better as a united front, with a plan in place."

My throat tightened, and tears pricked my eyes. They were right. And I was going nuts. The truth of what I might face in the dragons' mountain had made me lose my mind. But I had to be sharp and smart.

We had an army. We had to use it. And they had a right to fight for themselves.

I sucked in a ragged breath and nodded. "All right. You're all right. We should do this together. But we'll go according to my plan." If they didn't fight 'til the dragons woke, their chances were better.

"What do we do?" my mother asked.

My mind raced, coming up with a plan. With this many people, perhaps I could make a stab at rescuing my *deirfiúr* before I woke the dragons. That'd go even further toward ensuring their safety.

I looked out toward the crowd and called, "Can anyone create a portal?"

There was a rustling, and two women stepped forward. They were identical, with wild red hair and pale round cheeks. From the feel of their magic, they were from the Order of the Magica.

"Jenn and Alison," Claire whispered at my side. "Mercenaries with the Order."

"I can," said the one on the left. "I'm Jenn Donner. This is Alison Donner. Together, we can create a large portal going anywhere you like."

"Perfect. Thank you." I met the gazes of those in the crowd. More people had shown up, parking on the end of the street or appearing out of thin air. It was nearing our departure time, and the last of our reinforcements were arriving. A massive group appeared on silent feet—the vampires. Connor sprinted down the sidewalk from P & P, a bulging sack hanging from his side.

Once I was certain that everyone had arrived—though it was really just a guess—I raised my voice to carry over the crowd. Fortunately it was still dark and early. "Jenn and Alison will create the portal. I will go through first, along with my dragons. We will attempt to free my captured friends. While we are doing that, you will join us. It will be cold and dark and mountainous. The enemy is in a valley shaped like a bowl. You will arrive out of sight, but surround them in the mountains above. Once I have woken the dragons, you will flow down the mountainside to attack the demons within."

"What if you need help?" Ana asked. "Waking the dragons?"

I turned to her. "Only I can do that."

"I'll be with her," Ares said.

I wasn't even sure that he could accompany me to the dragons if there was a force field around them. He hadn't been able to pass the force field that cut off my village. But I didn't say anything—there was no time for arguments.

I met Ana's gaze. "The fight will begin when the dragons appear. Do you all agree?"

I needed their agreement on this. Anything else was too risky.

There was a sea of bobbing heads and a chorus of agreements.

"Thank you all," I said.

Claire pressed close and murmured, "No, thank you. Because you're going to do something dangerous, aren't you? Like, really dangerous."

I met her gaze, seeing the sad knowledge within. Ares hadn't figured it out. His fear for me had been abstract. Claire, my clever friend—she knew the sacrifice I thought I had to make. Her dark eyes shined with tears, but she blinked them back. If anyone knew the value of sacrifice, it was Claire.

I threw my arms around her and hugged her. "Take care of Cass and Del." I breathed the words, they were so quiet.

"Always." She squeezed hard, voice breaking.

I pulled back and didn't look at her. I couldn't. More than anything, I had to keep my shit together.

I turned to Connor, who stood a few feet back from his sister. "Do you have a couple of invisibility potions?"

"I do." He dug into his bag and then handed over the little vials.

I took them, holding on to his gaze a second too long. His brow wrinkled in question, but it wasn't like I could say anything like, "Oh yeah, just looking at you for the last time" without raising suspicion.

Because it might not be the last time. The forest sprite hadn't made it clear I would have to die to wake the dragons, though it was hard to think how I might give up every ounce of my magic and then want to live.

I turned from him and handed one of the vials to Ares. "Since I know you won't let me go alone."

He took it and smiled.

Jenn and Alison joined us.

"So, where's this portal going?" Alison asked. Her hair was topped with a green hat, but the rest spilled out, brilliant and red. It reminded me of Cass, and my heart ached.

"It's a place that's protected by primordial gods. It's hard to describe. Would it work if we took one of you there?"

"That's perfect," Jenn said. "We'll build the portal from both sides. That's strongest."

I turned to Ares, but my mother's voice stopped me.

I turned back to her. She approached, stopping to stand in front of me. She reached for my hands and squeezed.

"I'm proud of you, Nix." Her voice broke, but she sucked in a ragged breath and got herself under control. "Whatever you face, you are up to the task. And you *will* survive."

Did she guess my fears? Were they her own? I wasn't exactly a normal daughter, or a normal Magica. Of course my fate would be iffy. I possessed magic that was not my own, donated by the town that was willing to die to give it to me.

Was it so much of a stretch to think that I might die too?

Apparently my mother didn't think so, though she clearly—desperately—wanted to believe otherwise.

I hugged her, my throat too tight to speak. Finally, I managed to eek out an, "I love you."

"I love you too." Love and pride gleamed in her eyes.

My father stepped forward, and I repeated the motions, savoring the last moments with my parents. As soon as I pulled back from the hug, however, I shut down sentimentality. That would get me nowhere. Now was the time for action.

I wanted to thank the crowd, but really—it was condescending, wasn't it? They weren't fighting for me, but rather for themselves. For their loved ones and all the magic in the world. For the desire to live free from tyranny, out from underneath the boot of an evil madman.

Instead, I swept my gaze over the crowd and said, "I'll see you on the other side." I wasn't even sure if I would, but it didn't matter. I turned to Ares. "Can you take us now? To the rock outcropping where we hid before?"

He nodded and held out his hands. I took one, and Jenn took the other. A moment later, the ether sucked us in.

The air was bitter cold when we arrived, the night dark. There would be no dawn, not here in Svalbard at this time of year. Immediately, Jeff and the Pūķi appeared at my side. I smiled at them.

"Holy Merlin's balls, this is cold," Jenn said. "Where are we?"

"Svalbard, an island north of Norway." I inspected the terrain around us. Everything was silent and still. As I'd feared, the dragons' mountain was contained in a dome like the one that had surrounded my town. We'd have to break through that.

Jenn rubbed her hands together, then held them out. Magic glowed at her palms, a pale pink light that shined on the snow. The scent of the ocean swelled, bringing with it the sound of chirping birds.

Soon, the air in front of her began to shimmer, turning into a mirror. Then it disappeared entirely. Alison stood on the other side, her hands outstretched, a grin on her face. Then she stepped through.

Immediately, she scowled. "Cold as hell."

"That's what I said." Jenn hugged her sister, then turned to me. "Three at a time can come through, so you'd better give the order."

"You can," I said. "You're now in charge of transportation."

She saluted and grinned, then stepped through the portal.

I turned to Ares. "Ready?"

"What's the plan?"

"Get to the top of this mountain so we can see the valley below. Once we know where my *deirfiúr* are, and Aidan and Roarke, we take the invisibility potions. Then we sneak to them. They have to be in a blue cage like the one that held Alton, so I'll try to cut through it with my sword." I turned to Jeff and the Pūķi. "You guys come get us out of there when we're done. Stay hidden until we need you."

Jeff nodded, and the Pūķi just stared. But they got the picture. I knew how they worked at this point.

I eyed Jeff. He was pretty big now, the size of a large SUV. "Jeff, do you think you can be bigger?"

Magic swirled around him, silver and bright. Then he grew. And grew. Soon, he was the size of a small house.

"Shoot, Jeff." I grinned. "You can quit."

He snuffled happily, flame billowing from his nostrils.

"Just stay hidden, all right?" I said.

He nodded and flattened himself on the ground. I laughed. Fierce dragon sometimes, pretty much a goofy dog the rest of the time.

"Good luck," Alison said.

"Thanks. You too." I glanced at the portal, where people had started to flow through. "And remember, don't attack until the dragons are awake. That is *key*."

"How will we know?"

I thought of the massive dragons, envisioned them swooping through the sky. "Oh, you'll know."

Ares and I set off up the mountain, hiking in silence. Soon, my lungs and thighs burned. Snow made the going slow, but eventually we reached the crest. I got on my belly and shimmied forward, the cold snow sneaking down my jacket and making me shiver.

The sight below made my skin chill even more.

CHAPTER TWELVE

"Hundreds," I whispered. I couldn't see Drakon, but I could feel his magic, just a hint of it. He was here, somewhere.

"To the left." Ares pointed.

My gaze followed his arm. There, right beneath the dome that contained the dragons' mountain, was the blue cage trapping my *deirfiúr*. Like Alton, they stood frozen inside.

Rage welled inside me, dark and black. Fear, too, which tempered the heat of anger.

Unlike before, there was no lightning bolt connecting the cage to the dome. Rather, they butted right up against one another. I wouldn't be able to pull the same trick as last time, with cutting the connection. They were one and the same. Hopefully, if I woke the dragons, they could take care of it.

"We can't approach from the top or the sides," Ares said.

He was right. The top was covered by the dome, and the sides were too steep. We'd have to go straight through the army.

Smart, Drakon.

"I don't see Aidan or Roarke." Dread pierced me.

"I doubt they're dead," Ares said. "They're bargaining chips for your *deirfiúr*."

I clung to the thought, not sure how realistic it was but not caring. I needed to believe they were okay. That we'd get them out of here.

I tugged the vial of invisibility potion out of my pocket. Ares did the same. I uncorked it and drank the foul stuff, cringing at the muddy taste. The chill rushed over me and I disappeared. For half a second, I couldn't see Ares, then he appeared next to me.

I leaned over and kissed him hard. This was it for us, if I didn't survive. "I love you. Always."

He wrapped a hand around my neck and kissed me deeply, then pulled away. "I love you."

I nodded, tears prickling my eyes, then pulled away. Silently, we scrambled down the mountainside. Though we left tracks, it was a moonless night. As long as none of the demons studied the snow, we'd be okay.

There were so many below. A roiling sea of them. All species, all kinds of magical signatures, all feeling like darkness and evil. I shuddered as their magic washed over me. The things these demons could do with their magic....

Shouldn't be allowed on Earth.

As we neared the valley, the raucous sounds of demons filled the air. They partied and fought and argued, none of them seeming to sleep. Dozens of fires burned, with demons surrounding each one. It looked like an ancient battlefield the night before the fight.

But these were the bad guys.

My heart lodged in my throat as we reached the bottom of the valley. From down here, the crush of demons looked impenetrable. They were packed in like sardines. Their magic made me gag.

Ares reached for my hand and squeezed, then let go and led the way. We wove between the crowds of demons, careful not to touch anyone. The hair on my arms stood on end as we snuck by a group that searched the air where we stood.

Could they see us?

A demon sprawled in front of me, dead or passed out, I couldn't tell. Ares stepped over. I jumped.

We were halfway across when the crowd crushed in around us. They were on all sides, pressing ever closer. They were all watching something that I was too short to see. There were shouts and jeers. The smacking of fists. They were crowded around a fight to the left. I edged away.

"Oy, what you doin'?"

I stiffened at the rough voice and turned. A demon raked his gaze over me. He could *see* me. Fear spiked in my chest. But none of the other demons seemed to notice. All their gazes were riveted on whatever had formed this crowd.

Could this demon see through invisibility potions?

"Oy."

I didn't let him finish. Just conjured a dagger and sank it into his heart. I'd never moved so fast in my life. The demon gurgled, but made no other noise. Ares appeared a millisecond later, grabbing the demon's body and lowering him to the ground.

The crush of demons around us was so fierce that no one seemed to notice. Tension tightened my muscles as we left him where he lay and hurried off. *Please don't let us get caught.*

We were about twenty yards away when the shouts started up. Someone had found him. But it seemed that no one saw us.

"We're close," Ares whispered.

"How close?" I craned my neck. I could see the cage containing my *deirfiúr* because it was on higher ground, but not the edge of the demon army. We were still in the thick of it, as far as I could tell.

"Twenty yards." He gripped my hand and led me through the crowd.

When we reached the edge, I sucked in a breath of sweet, fresh air. The slope led upward toward the glowing blue cage. It was a dome, like Alton's had been, and Cass and Del stood frozen within.

My heart ached to see them like that. I burned to race up the mountainside toward them, but we had to be smart.

"Go from the side," Ares said.

I nodded my agreement. We edged along the crowd of demons, toward an emptier area. There'd be fewer demons to see our footprints in the snow over here. We'd just have to pray they didn't look.

As fast as I could, I raced up the mountainside. Del and Cass were a couple hundred yards up, and my lungs burned by the time I reached their elevation. Once I did, I hurried toward them, Ares at my side. Tension tightened every muscle as I waited for a demon from below to spot our footsteps, or for my invisibility potion to wear off.

No one shouted.

The magic of the dome burned my skin as I approached. I shuddered. I'd never felt anything like this, and didn't want to ever again. The electric blue of the cage bars pulsed with light as I neared.

"Del, Cass!" I whispered.

They didn't move, but I thought maybe I saw something in their eyes.

"I'm going to get you out!" I drew my sword from the ether and raised it high overhead. With a quick prayer to the fates, I brought it crashing down on the blue cage.

Electricity shot up my arms. I flew backward and landed hard in the snow. Light flashed.

Blinking, pain racing through me, I scrambled to my feet.

My *deirfiúr* were still trapped.

Shit!

I stumbled toward the cage, raising my sword and slicing down.

Boom!

I was thrown backward again, electricity singing through me. I surged up.

"They're still trapped." Ares rose beside me. Apparently he'd been thrown back as well.

And he was right. The cage was still intact. My *deirfiúr* still frozen.

"Drakon has changed the magic." Panic surged in my chest. Had he imbued it with some of his own strength? My blade didn't work on that. "My sword worked before."

"He's smart."

A roar sounded from below. The demons were charging up the mountainside, straight for us. My attempts on the cage had alerted them. My heart leapt into my throat. They were only a hundred yards away.

A screech rent the night air, chilling my skin.

"Drakon." I raised the sword one last time, desperate, and sliced down on the cage. Electricity threw me backwards. Pain sang. I dragged myself up.

The cage was still there. My *deirfiúr* still wrapped.

The demons were closer, bearing down on us.

And in the sky above, Drakon raced for us. He was still several hundred yards off, but gaining.

"Jeff!" I screamed, praying he could find us despite our invisibility. My gaze raced back to my trapped *deirfiúr*. My heart broke in my chest, pain like I'd never known.

I had to leave them.

If my blade couldn't free them, then only one thing could— the dragons.

Jeff swooped from the sky, the size of a house. He landed with a heavy thud in the snow. Thank fates his magic had allowed him to see us.

Jeff turned to face the oncoming demons. The first wave was only forty yards away. He roared, breathing a massive jet of fire on them. They clambered backwards, some of them alight.

I climbed onto his back, Ares behind me.

"Go!" I screamed.

Jeff launched himself into the air. I clung to his back as the cold wind pulled at my hair and stung my eyes.

In the distance, the red Pūki tried to distract Drakon, shooting flames at his eyes. I leaned over Jeff's back and peered into the valley below. An open circle in the middle of the crowd caught my eye. Two men were tied within—Roarke and Aidan. They were conscious at least, tied to a pole. The demons around them jeered and screamed, but they couldn't reach them for some reason. A force field, maybe. Ares had been right though—they were being saved for something. Whatever use Drakon had for my *deirfiúr* and their men ... No way I was letting it happen.

I pointed and screamed. "That way!"

At least I could save them before I went into the mountain. Jeff swooped toward them. I turned back to Ares. I didn't even have to ask.

He nodded and kissed me hard. Jeff plunged low over our friends, and Ares leapt off his back, landing right next to Roarke. No one could see him but me, though Roarke and Aidan jerked, clearly able to hear that something was up.

As Jeff flew away, I watched Ares cut their bonds with his shadow sword. It took several tries—possibly to cut through magic as well—but eventually the men burst free.

Immediately, they shifted. A dark gray tornado formed around Roarke. His dark wings flared wide, and he lunged into the sky. Golden light glowed from Aidan, then the massive griffon stood in his place. Ares leapt upon his back, and they flew high into the night.

A shriek from my right forced me to look away.

Drakon was fighting his way toward me, but the Pūki were trying to hold him off. Three more figures pelted him with blasts of light. I squinted, trying to make out their forms in the dim light.

Three flying horses, each ridden by a woman in armor. One wore gold, one silver, and one opal.

The goddesses of fate. Laima, Karta, and Dekla had made their way here.

For the first time, hope surged in my chest. No matter what happened to me, we'd be victorious here today. We had to be. The goddesses of fate fought on our side.

"To the back of the dome!" I cried to Jeff. There was no time to race along through the tunnel. It, too, was surrounded by the dome, so it wasn't a shortcut. We'd have to go straight in.

Jeff flew toward the dome, looking for a place to land. Magic and power flowed through me, coming straight from my dragon. He did make me stronger, as Fiona had said he would.

Jeff climbed high in the air. I looked down, catching sight of my friends perched on the mountainsides that ringed the valley, hidden. Waiting to attack. It was possible Drakon might see them from the air. I'd have to be fast.

Jeff climbed higher. I caught sight of another valley.

It was full of demons. Demons we hadn't seen. Fear turned my blood to ice. There were twice the enemies as we'd thought, outnumbering us now.

No. No. No.

My success was vital. I had to wake the dragons now. It'd always been necessary, but this made it even more so. To have any hope of survival, my friends needed the dragons fighting on their side.

And they needed them quickly. I had to get through the dome. But if my blade hadn't cut through the electric blue cage, would it work on the dome? It was probably made of stronger stuff as well.

My mind raced. How was I going to do this?

Jeff neared the dome, clearly looking for a place to land.

But maybe we shouldn't land.

I needed Jeff's strength. His power.

"Hover near the dome!" I cried.

Jeff flew close. I leaned over his side, reaching out with my blade. I struck, stabbing hard into the smoky barrier.

"Fly forward!"

Jeff followed my command, flying along the dome. I kept my blade sunk into the black mist, tearing a hole in the barrier that was big enough to fit us both. His magic had helped—no question.

From there, Jeff knew what to do. He plunged through the barrier, going straight through the weak spot. I shuddered as we passed through, then I was in the darkened interior of the mountain.

The white light shined up from below, beckoning.

"Down!" I called.

Jeff flew down. I clung to his back, heart pounding. He landed on a ledge between the silver and black dragons. This was right where I'd stood when I'd watched my *deirfiúr* be abducted. The dragons were still dead asleep.

I climbed off Jeff's back, then walked around to his face. I touched his cheek and looked into his black eyes. He was just so big now, but I could still see the little dragon there. "I love you, Jeff. I always will."

He snuffled, his nose blowing warm air all over me.

I smiled. "Now go help my friends. And be safe."

Confusion glinted in his onyx eyes.

"Go." I hardened my voice. "They need you. Be ready to pick up Cass and Del when they are freed."

Understanding shined in his eyes. He nodded, then took off, flying back up through the mountain and slipping through the tear that I'd created.

Suddenly, I felt so alone.

The dragons were no company. They were so deeply asleep that they might as well be dead.

But that was the whole reason I was here. To see to it that they wouldn't die. I looked at the three of them, the source of all magic, and couldn't help but be awed all over again. I focused on that awe as I stepped toward the edge of the pit.

White magic and light flowed up, feeding the dragons.

But it wasn't enough.

Because I possessed the rest of that magic. I was life. Not just for me and not just for the world, but for the dragons as well. All the magic that Elesius had given me wasn't for *me*. I was just a custodian.

I still wasn't sure how I was supposed to give them my magic —Elesius's magic—but instinct drove me to hold out my hands, directing them at the glowing pit below.

Tears rolled down my cheeks as I forced my magic out of myself. I envisioned it as liquid pouring from my fingertips, falling into the light below.

My village had sacrificed for me, and I would sacrifice for the dragons. For the world. This magic had never been mine, but theirs.

Weakness stole over me as the magic poured out of me. Was Elesius growing weak as well? Without me to help it grow, would it die fully?

Was I sacrificing my village as well as myself?

Pain lanced me at the thought, but I remembered my mother. She was obsessed with the choice, and she'd made hers. Elesius had made theirs. As I would save the dragons, so, too, would they. *Because* of them, I would save the dragons.

I forced more magic out of myself, my muscles trembling. According to the laws of magic as I knew them, this shouldn't be possible. But I was standing in an impossible place, doing an impossible thing.

Possible meant nothing.

The air sparked around me as my magic flowed into the pit, and then into the dragons. I could see it pulsing as a white light, no longer my own. Soon, I could hardly stand. Weakness flowed through me. I forced more magic out. More. More.

But the dragons didn't wake.

Finally, there was nothing left to give. Or at least, whatever was left was so small it couldn't find its way out of me.

And still, the dragons slept. The energy in the air was stronger. They looked stronger. But they slept on.

Tears poured down my face. It wasn't enough. *I* wasn't enough.

I dragged in a ragged breath.

Or was I?

Was I only giving it half? Did I need to give everything, even my life?

My mind calmed.

It was obvious, wasn't it? I hadn't wanted to believe the forest spirit, but she'd been clear. I had to become one with them. Or my magic did, at least.

I dragged in a ragged breath and said goodbye to Cass and Del. Their faces flashed in my mind's eye. Memories. I said goodbye to Ares. My parents. Aidan and Roarke, Connor and Claire. Mordaca, Aerdeca, Dr. Garriso. All of them, their names in my head, I stepped off the ledge.

This time, nothing rose up to meet me.

Wind tore at my hair as I fell, plummeting into the light. But my mind was calm, my heart convinced.

I didn't understand this magic, but I didn't have to.

When the white flames engulfed me, the pain was sharp, but brief. It tore through my bones and muscles. But right before my world went black, I heard the dragons roar, and I smiled.

CHAPTER THIRTEEN

Light exploded behind my eyes. Power surged through me, foreign and strange. My body felt wrong.

But instinct drove my muscles, my mind. I moved my arms, realizing only then that I no longer had arms.

I had wings. Brilliant red wings, tipped with yellow feathers.

I was a phoenix.

Lightness and joy tore through me. I flapped my new wings, clumsy at first, in the middle of this bright white light, then stronger. Fiercer.

I shot from the light, following my instinct toward the sky.

Was this real?

Did I care?

Not even a little. I pushed my new body, flying toward the darkness above. Flying was *amazing.* I felt so strong, so free. The roar of dragons echoed from above. Calling to me. I followed their cry, shooting up from the pit and into the mountain cavern.

The dragons no longer slept. The ledges were empty. My heart soared as I flew for the top of the mountain. I shot out into the sky. Drakon's barrier was broken—no doubt by the dragons.

The aurora borealis shone bright in the sky—purple, green,

yellow. It highlighted the two dragons who swooped through the night, diving for the demons below. It was impossible not to notice them—they were terrifying and beautiful. Power incarnate, lunging toward the demons below and blasting them with their brilliant red flame. There were only two dragons, though. Where was the third?

I didn't know how long I'd been—dead?—but the battle raged in the valley and on the mountainside. I swept up into the air, taking in my surroundings. The mountainside teemed with my allies, racing down through the snow to collide with the enemy in the valley below. The demons roared and ran for them, brandishing weapons and throwing bursts of flame and magic.

I sought my *deirfiúr*, but their blue magic cage was gone. It had happened when the dragons had destroyed the barrier, most likely.

Cass and Del were gone as well. Demons crowded in their place, as if they'd raced for the captives when the cage had been destroyed. Fear chilled me. I dived low, flying over the place where their cage had been. Demons trampled the ground, but I saw no sign of them.

I shoved aside the fear. They couldn't be dead. I would *feel* that.

Drakon was nowhere to be seen, but perhaps he was in the other valley. As I flew that direction, hoping to find him, I inspected the battle below.

From the mountain to the west, the shifters pounded down into the valley. Bears, tigers, wolves, and dogs. All variety of predators raced toward the demons. The clash was fierce, with the biggest animals going straight for the demons' throats. An orange house cat rode on the back of a bear, straight for a demon the size of a football player. A house cat?

Even as a phoenix, I realized that this was seriously weird. The battle animals were usually large predators, like the lions. As the bear neared the demon, he turned right, headed for another enemy. The cat leapt off the bear's back, fangs glinting in the light of the aurora. It landed on the demon's chest, sinking its fangs into the neck. Blood sprayed. The demon roared. The cat chomped again.

I could *hear* it.

My senses were incredible. I had to be two hundred yards away, but I could hear that specific fight because I focused on it.

No longer worried for the cat—*that* cat could handle himself —I swooped low over the battle. The mercenaries from the Order of the Magica were on the eastern slope, launching coordinated attacks against the demons in the valley below. They lobbed massive balls of fire and sonic booms, bowling over the enemy. They used their positioning to their advantage, hiding behind conjured barricades. I didn't see Claire with her colleagues.

Please be with Cass and Del.

Her loyalty was to us first, so odds were good that she was with them and not already downed.

Movement through the demons in the valley caught my eye. A large vehicle drove through the crowd, plowing the demons aside.

Ana and Bree!

Ana drove the modified buggy. It had larger tires—for the snow?—and a cage around the cockpit. Bree hung off the platform in the back, wielding a sword like a madwoman. She was wild, slicing at the demons with more enthusiasm than skill. But it worked. Blood flew as she cut them down. Ana shrieked every time she hit a demon, a bloodcurdling war cry.

Why didn't they use their magic?

Did they even have it anymore?

I couldn't wonder, not when I had to find my *deirfiúr*. And it wasn't like it mattered—I couldn't stop them. They threw themselves into the fray anyway, going to the most dangerous spots— right in the middle of the demons.

I flew toward the other valley, the one right on the other side of the mountain. Before I crested the mountain, I caught sight of a giant creature rampaging through the demons.

Emile and Prince Louie. The Animus Mage rode his giant two-headed dog. I hadn't seen the beast in months, but it was plowing through demons like they were kibble. The canine monster was twenty feet tall, and each head was different. One was that of a golden retriever, the other that of a white poodle. The poodle's eyes were cloudy, and its breath was green gas, a deadly poison that I'd once gotten a horrible whiff of.

Prince Louie was having the time of his life as he chomped on demons, though Emile looked more serious as he directed the dog through the enemy. Ralph and Rufus, the two little rats, rode on his shoulder, their whiskers twitching in the wind.

I couldn't get over my new senses. To see rat whiskers from this distance ... It was incredible.

As I neared the other valley, I finally caught sight of one of my friends. Roarke. He stood with Alison and Jenn, the two portal mages. Magic shimmered in the air as they worked, their hands outstretched and light glowing brightly. Roarke was touching each of their shoulder's, as if giving them guidance. In where to place the portal? But demons were charging toward them. Roarke didn't stop what he was doing to defend, so I dove, tilting my wings to clip a row of demons.

I was pretty sure I was big enough to do damage—it was hard to say, really—but it seemed to work. The demons flew backward, as if shocked by the feel of my feathers. Did I deliver electricity?

"Thanks!" The voice was feminine. Jenn or Alison, I wasn't sure.

I swooped and dove, buying them time to finish their portal. If Roarke was there, they had to be creating a portal to the Underworld. To drive the demons back to hell?

So smart.

We could kill every single one of them, and they'd wake up in hell anyway. But if we built a portal and herded them in....

So much faster and less dangerous.

I grinned—or at least, I thought I did since it was hard to tell with a beak—and snuck a peek. Through the portal, I saw a flaming red hellscape.

Yep, genius.

"We're done!" Roarke waved, his face confused as he studied me. Then delight spread across his features.

Did he know me?

I screeched in greeting, then wheeled off and flew over the mountain. The second valley looked much like the first, and I was grateful for the number of warriors who had volunteered.

My family and the people of Elesius rode horses along the edges of the valley, striking at the demons within. My mother and father rode side by side, slicing their swords with precision. It was a bloodbath near them. An outrider protected my parents from any demons who threw long-range spells, blocking the magic so the fighters could cut down the enemy. In fact, there were many magic blockers amongst my mother's people. They worked as a team—blockers and fighters. Was this how so many had survived the last battle?

It was genius.

Near them, the vampires fought under the light of the aurora. Thank fates we had that and not the sun. Doyen and Magisteria led the charge, racing through the demons and obliterating them with their shadow swords. They swung with such strength that heads flew into the air, bouncing off of other fighters. It was gruesome, but the vampires seemed to love it. The League of FireSouls fought alongside them, fierce in their burnished red armor.

I ignored them all, searching the sky for Drakon or my friends.

First, I saw the third dragon. The white one swooped over the demons, barbecuing them like he was preparing for a picnic. Beyond the white dragon, a shadowy form glinted in the light of the aurora. They were far off, hundreds of yards away on the other side of the valley, but it was Drakon and my friends.

I screeched and flew toward them, racing through the sky as the wind tore at my feathers. Drakon was *chasing* Cass and Del. He couldn't return them to their cage, so it had to be vengeance. Cass was in her griffon form, bigger and stronger than I'd ever seen her. Del, as a phantom, rode on her back. As Cass raced away from Drakon, Del leaned back and fired massive icicles at him.

Drakon was fast, ducking away from the projectiles. But every now and again she hit him. Aidan, as a massive golden griffon, swooped around Drakon, going for the eyes. He slowed the bastard, but Drakon was still fast. And mostly impervious to the blows of my friends.

On the mountainside nearest them, Connor and Claire stood. Claire fired massive fireballs. Like Del, she only occasionally hit Drakon. While Drakon might roar and falter, he kept going. Connor shot potion bombs using some strange contraption I'd never seen before. They sailed hundreds of yards through the air, slamming into Drakon.

The Pūķi dived around as well—each carrying a *rider?* Mordaca and Aerdeca directed the red dragons to fly in front of Drakon, getting between him and my *deirfiúr*. They positioned themselves in front of him but to the sides. Wind tore at their hair as they each sliced their palms, then held out their hands. A massive bolt of lightning formed between them, an electric wall that Drakon plowed into.

He crashed through the barrier, then flailed and roared, finally righting himself and charging on.

I suddenly realized—Cass and Del weren't running from him. They were leading him toward dangers. They hoped that with all their strength combined, they could beat Drakon.

But where were Ares and Jeff?

I searched as I flew for Drakon, finally catching sight of Jeff near my parents. A massive demon—a giant, actually—was charging toward them. The creature was thirty feet tall, with spikes all down its back and a massive spiked club in his hand. He swung it high, clearly aiming for my parents, the leaders of that faction.

Ares and Jeff raced toward the beast, colliding with him right before he brought the club down on my mother. Ares leapt off Jeff, landing on the giant's shoulder. He swiped out with his shadow sword as Jeff flew into the air, catching sight of me.

My dragon shrieked with joy, racing toward me. My heart swelled as the green and red blur streaked for me, but I screeched back at him, demanding he return to Ares. As if he understood, Jeff turned and swooped back toward the vampire.

I left them, nearly to Drakon now. I'd been flying blind, my eyes too riveted to Ares, and I was nearly upon them all. The scene was much the same, with my friends attacking and Drakon rebuffing. He was nearly to Cass and Del.

I pushed myself faster, racing toward him, colliding with his side.

He roared as an electric shock tore through him, and he tumbled end over end. There was a sizzling black hole where my beak had pierced.

Only the beak of the phoenix can defeat Drakon.

That's what Athena had said.

And that's how I would defeat him. Not with my sword, but with my new form. Life would defeat the beast who sought to be death.

Drakon righted himself. His black gaze met mine, rage burning in the depths of his eyes. He hissed, angry and ... scared?

Then he turned and fled, a coward.

To live and fight another day?

No way.

I shrieked and flew after him, but he was fast. Too fast. I might be strong, but a shadow dragon beat a phoenix any day. At least for speed.

As if they'd heard my call, my friends rallied. The white dragon popped its head up, catching my gaze. Then it hurtled toward Drakon, hovering to the east, blocking his way. From the west, the three fates appeared. Laima, Dekla, and Karta, each riding a winged horse, formed a barrier with their magic. It glowed bright, a swirling mix of their gold, silver, and opal.

As if he knew he couldn't pass them, Drakon raced for the south, away from me.

But Connor and Claire were waiting, along with Cass and Del, who'd landed on the mountain ridge next to them. Cass was in her human form again. She yelled at Claire, something about a barrier. They raised their hands, fire blasting from their palms, and formed a fiery wall in the sky. Connor hurled a potion bomb at the flame. It exploded, green and bright, providing fuel that made the fire rise hundreds of feet high.

Roarke hovered above, along with Aerdeca and Mordaca on the Pūķi, who formed another electric barrier. Jeff and Ares joined them, completing the cage.

Drakon could only go down. Or come for me.

He roared his rage, then whirled on the air, racing for me. He hurtled toward me like a freight train, steam billowing from his nostrils. Rage gleamed in his eyes and vibrated along his body.

The briefest frisson of fear streaked through me. He might not want to fight me, but that didn't mean he couldn't win.

I shrieked my battle cry and flew for him. I ducked my head right before we collided, going for his chest. We slammed together, spinning in midair. The force was an explosion. Pain surged through me, but not nearly as bad as when I'd been human. Drakon thrashed with the electric shock of my blow. We both zapped each other, but my magic was stronger now.

My beak had plowed into his chest, leaving a gaping wound, but I hadn't hit his heart.

Drakon roared and tore away, flying upward. I chased, eyeing his chest and the beating black heart within. He neared the barrier above, Ares, Aidan, Aerdeca, and Mordaca all waiting for him, then turned around and dove for me.

I pushed myself faster. There would be no failure.

As he neared, I dodged, my beak going unerringly for his heart. It beckoned me, so easy to see. His claws tore into my wing, but my beak found its mark. I struck fast and hard, plucking the black organ from his chest.

Electricity surged through me, shaking my bones and making pain dance in front of my eyes. I chomped down on his heart.

It exploded into dust.

Then Drakon exploded into dust.

Victory surged through me. I spat out the dust and shot high into the sky, spinning on the air. All around, I saw my friends. Without them, I wouldn't have succeeded. We wouldn't have succeeded. They had tired him out, then trapped him so I could finish the job. Our troops and the dragons had kept the demons from launching an air attack at us.

Together, we'd done it.

I caught their gazes briefly—joy and fear. Afraid I wouldn't turn back to human?

I couldn't think of that now. Instead, I plowed back down to the fray. My friends joined. Most of the demons were dead, their earthly bodies nothing but crisped flesh from the dragons or riddled with wounds from our warriors. Their souls would be back in hell by now.

At the edge of the valley, I caught sight of Roarke, Jenn, and Alison. They'd just finished creating a second portal in this valley.

Perfect.

I swooped low, starting at the opposite side of the valley, and herded the demons to the portal. My friends joined me, Jeff flying along joyfully and shooting flame at their butts. Ares, on Jeff's back, couldn't stop looking at me, awe on his face.

Once the demons caught sight of the portal and figured out what we were doing, they actually helped, racing for the exit. Though they probably didn't want to go back to hell, it was pretty clear by now that we were going to win. So they might as well save themselves the misery of death here on Earth.

Once the final demon had been rushed into the portal, a cry of victory rose up, echoing through the mountains. The fighters in the other valley joined in. I flew high into the sky, peering over the mountaintops. That valley was safe too. All the demons dead or gone.

I swept the field with my keen gaze. Though there were wounded, there didn't appear to be a lot of ours dead. Our plan had worked. The dragons had sent the demons into a tailspin, making it easier and safer for our fighters. I flew low over the nearest valley, searching out my friends.

They stood in the middle of the trampled snow. Blood splattered the white stuff, but the demon bodies were already disappearing.

I landed with a *thud* next to Cass and Del, still not used to this new form.

"Nix?" Tears poured down Cass's face.

Del ran for me, throwing herself against my feathered chest. Her head reached to my neck. I realized with a shock that I was a lot smaller than I'd realized. Much smaller than Drakon had been.

Good thing I hadn't known that at the time.

I wanted to hug my *deirfiúr*. My parents. Ares. All my friends.

Could I?

Not with wings, at least.

I envisioned my human form, praying that I could change back. I'd died.

Definitely.

So could I come back?

Magic thrummed through me, the familiar feeling of life rushing through my veins. The same magic that had made the grass grow in Elesius also ran through me. Silver light sparkled in the air around me, and I shrank.

I had arms!

"Nix!" Cass threw her arms around Del and me.

I hugged them back, tears pouring down my cheeks. I hadn't died! And I wasn't stuck as a phoenix. Better yet, I'd transformed back to human while still wearing my clothes.

Not that it hadn't been ridiculously cool to be a phoenix, but I didn't want to spend the rest of my life screeching at people and hoping they understood. Also, I liked having thumbs.

I pulled back from my *deirfiúr*, my gaze racing around to take everyone in. All of my friends were alive. Many sported injuries, were bleeding and limping, but everyone was standing.

"What happened?" Cass demanded.

"Seems pretty obvious," Del said wryly. "Only one way you turn into a phoenix."

Cass nodded, understanding glinting in her eyes. "We felt it, you know. A terrible pain. I wasn't sure what it was, but I was scared."

"It didn't last, though," Del said. "Calm came over me. Then you appeared. As a freaking bird."

"Phoenix," I insisted. "Much cooler."

Cass and Del laughed.

Ares slipped through the crowd toward me, wrapped his arms around me, and hugged me close. I leaned into him, absorbing his warmth and so glad to be with him.

"So Aethelred was right," Ares murmured. "I did lose what I loved most. I felt it too, when you died. My world stopped."

The aching pain in his voice made me hug him tight. "Did you feel when I came back?"

"I did." He kissed the top of my head. "Then I saw you."

"Cool, huh?" I pulled back to look at his face.

He just smiled and nodded, then kissed my forehead. There'd be time to talk later.

"Nix!" my mother's voice called from behind.

I pulled away from Ares. She and my father galloped their horses toward us. My mother leapt off her stallion and raced toward me to drag me in for a big hug.

"You did it!" she cried against my hair.

"We all did it." I looked at her. Tears streamed down her face. My father stood next to her. He reached out and gripped my shoulder. I smiled at him. "We all did it. Without Elesius, I wouldn't have had the magic to give the dragons."

"You did everything right," my mother said. "I'm so proud."

"*We're* so proud," my father said.

I grinned, but the sound of whooshing air distracted me. I looked up. My jaw dropped.

The three enormous dragons hovered overhead, blocking out the aurora. They gleamed in the firelight that Cass and Claire had set up around us, their scales shining.

Then they landed all around us, towering like houses. A shiver raced over me. Fear and awe combined. Cass and Del sidled closer to me until our shoulders touched.

The dragons leaned their large heads down until they were eye to eye with the three of us. Their eyes gleamed, green, blue, and purple. Steam wafted from their noses.

They could barbecue us in a second, but they wouldn't. Still, I couldn't help but think it. I'd have to be a moron not to think it.

The dragons touched their noses almost to ours. For one blissful moment, I thought that I understood them. That they said thank you.

"Thank you," I echoed it back to them. We may have saved them, but they'd saved us in return.

The dragons snuffled warm air that billowed over our faces

and smelled of fire, then took off into the night sky. They swept off through the aurora, their bodies gleaming in the light.

"Where are they going?" my mother asked.

"I have no idea." But at least they weren't in the mountain anymore. And they were safe.

Magic was safe.

CHAPTER FOURTEEN

For the first time in months, I sat at the desk in Ancient Magic. I'd spent the entire day here, dusting the place while waiting for people to figure out we were once again open.

After the excitement of the last few months, it was almost eerily quiet to be back in my normal life, tending the desk and protecting the wares.

But it was a good kind of quiet. The kind I'd chosen for myself. And soon enough, demons or other bandits would try to break in and steal the magic from our shelves. Little did they know that I could now turn into a phoenix and chomp their heads off.

But I didn't look forward to it. I *really* wouldn't mind if there wasn't any drama for a while. I had a life to catch up on. And if I wanted some excitement, I could join Cass and Del on an artifact-hunting mission.

"Is this a real Ming vase?" asked the man who stood in the corner. He'd entered the shop about twenty minutes ago and had been browsing since then.

"No. Just a replica. But the magic inside is legit. Once housed in a real Ming vase, if that helps any."

He shrugged, then put down the vase.

Fine by me. If this dude wanted real artifacts, we couldn't help him with that. It was illegal, and we didn't deal in that shit. He continued to browse, finally settling on a small locket containing a concealment charm. I rang him up, then he was out the door right before Cass and Del came in.

They were windblown and red-cheeked, still looking out of breath. My eyes riveted on the box in their hands.

"You get it?" I came out from behind the desk.

"In the nick of time," Del said. "The magic feels really unstable in this one."

It'd been two days since the battle with Drakon. We'd gotten back to normal life quickly, with Del and Cass going out to hunt an artifact for the shop today. All was right with the world.

Cass pushed her red hair back from her face and looked at the clock over the desk. "Almost five. Time for drinks with Connor and Claire. They invited us over. You want to wait to transfer the magic?"

I shook my head. "Nah. I'd like to do it now. A little piece of real life. Then you can take the original back to the site tomorrow."

"And with Drakon dead, no one will come after it and destroy the site." Cass grinned. "Thank God the bastard is dead."

"No kidding." I took the box from her and carried it to the desk. "I just can't believe it's all over."

Cass and Del followed me, stopping at the front of the desk while I walked behind.

"It's been a long year," Del said. "The three of us, with our three tasks. But I think the Triumvirate can have a break now."

"After what we just went through—after what Nix just went through, jumping into that pit—I think we all deserve a break," Cass said.

"And this was the first day of the rest of our lives. Our *normal* lives." I opened the box and revealed the wide silver bracelet.

Magic radiated from it. It was silver with a blue glint, a bit like one of the dragons. I smiled at the memory of the beasts. "I can't believe dragons are flying through the world now."

"At least there's been no news stories about humans freaking out," Cass said.

"Seriously. There are enough about the supernaturals going nuts." It'd been all over the news.

"I don't think humans can see them," Del said. "It's the only thing that makes sense."

"And thank fates for that. Dragons would really blow our cover." If they could see the dragons, it'd be impossible for humans not to realize that magic was real.

"So all is well with the world." Cass grinned. "Thanks to us."

"No time for modesty, I see," Del said.

"Ha." Cass laughed. "As if I have time for modesty after what we've been through."

"Though I do wonder what the Order will say," Del said. "Or the Alpha Council. They had no idea that such bad shit was going down. Not until they showed up for the final battle."

I shivered. They still didn't know what we were. But some of their mercenaries had to have seen me transform from a phoenix. That alone was weird magic, and the Order didn't like weird, unfamiliar magic.

"I can't imagine we'd be in trouble," Cass said. "Not after all we've done."

"I hope you're right." The Order had never been very logical though. But I couldn't focus on that now. I wanted to live in the present—in the amazing life we'd saved for ourselves.

And the present meant transferring the magic from this bracelet to a replica. Because Cass was right. The magic in the bracelet was old and *really* unstable. Felt like it was going to blow any minute.

First, I conjured a replica—an identical silver bracelet made of one wide piece of metal. Then I hovered my hand over the original. Blue light glowed as I drew the magic out, then transferred it over to the bracelet. It felt good to be back to normal life.

When the magic had flowed into the replica, I removed my hand and smiled, satisfied. "That's a cool one. I think it will repel any spell if the wearer holds it up."

"Like Wonder Woman's arm bands," Del said.

"Kinda. But silver. And for spells." Actually, I really liked the thing. I ran my fingertips over the bracelet. Maybe I'd keep it.

"Ready?" Cass asked. "It's already after five. Time for drinks!"

I shook my head, the spell broken. "Yeah. Ares is supposed to meet us there."

"You're in loooove." Del grinned as I put the two bracelets on the shelf behind the desk.

I shot her a wry look. "So are you, dummy. And this isn't fifth grade."

"No." She smiled wider and shook her head. "But I'm just happy, is all. Happy that everything is fine. We've feared for our lives for months. Death lurked around every corner. And now it's over."

I looped my arm with hers and followed her outside, stopping to turn around and ignite the charm that protected the shop. When I was done, Cass looped her arm around mine.

The three of us walked arm in arm down the sidewalk. It was already dark because it was the dead of winter, but the street-lights cast a warm glow over Factory Row.

Our home was safe, and I couldn't help but admire every inch of it. Everything was back to normal. True, I did have to pay back Artemis by helping her find something, but other than that, all my obligations were complete.

The familiar glow of P & P spilled out onto the sidewalk, welcoming us forward. As we neared the glass windows, I realized it wasn't nearly as empty as I'd expected. I'd been antici-pating just a few friends ... but it was everyone.

We walked through the door as everyone shouted, "Surprise!"

"It's not my birthday," I said.

"Kinda is." Claire stepped forward. "You were born as a phoenix a couple days ago."

It was so wonderful to see all of my friends smiling and laughing and just plain old not dead that I shrugged and grinned. "Okay!"

Claire handed me a glass of Four Roses, while Connor passed a PBR to Cass and a mug of red wine to Del.

Before I could speak, everyone raised their glasses. "To the Triumvirate!"

Jeff, who hovered in the air as a small dragon once again, blew a blast of flame in celebration.

My eyes teared up. "Thanks, guys."

Cass and Del mirrored the sentiment. We met each other's gazes, then we all drank.

From the corner, Magisteria and Doyen raised their glasses to me. Dr. Garriso, too. All the FireSouls. Aerdeca and Mordaca, who were once again dressed in their signature black and white.

Ares came over to hug me. I leaned against him and sipped my bourbon, enjoying being around my friends. The night passed in song and gaiety. Around ten o'clock, Cass, Del, and I were standing near the open door for a breath of fresh air when an unfamiliar man walked in.

I turned to face him, catching sight of the badge on his jacket.

Order of the Magica.

I swallowed hard. He wore the neatly pressed suit of a courier. His gaze landed on the three of us, recognition flaring.

"Just who I was looking for." He handed out an envelope. "You've been summoned."

"Summoned?" Cass asked.

With a shaking hand, I took the envelope.

Claire bustled up behind us. "Richard, what is this?"

The courier turned to face Claire. "Claire. I'm just delivering a message from the Order."

"I get that, but this is a private party." She hustled him to the door. "It could have waited."

Out on the sidewalk, he turned to face us. His dark hair gleamed in the light, and his expression was sober. "It really couldn't wait."

I opened the envelope, revealing a thick piece of parchment. My breath held as my eyes raced over the script. "It's a summons to the council chambers. At eight tomorrow."

Del's pale face met mine. "Why?"

"Doesn't say."

"They must know what we are." Cass's voice shook slightly. "We've used so much crazy magic lately."

"Yeah, but they already knew we are capable of crazy magic," Del said. "Their mercenaries have seen us use it before. That doesn't mean they know what we are."

"But they've never called us for a meeting before," I said. "This is different."

Our identity as FireSouls was a secret. It was no longer as closely guarded as it had once been—the trials we'd faced these last months had ensured that—but we didn't need to be walking into the council chambers of the Order of the Magica with that secret potentially out in the open. Still....

"We have to go," I said. "It's not guaranteed that it will be bad."

"No, you don't have to go." My mother's voice sounded from behind me. "You can come live with us."

I turned to her. "We can't run any longer. I fought hard for this life here in Magic's Bend. As much as I love visiting you, this is my home now. I can't run."

She smiled, nodding her understanding.

"I agree," Cass said

"No more running," Del said.

"I'll go with you," Ares said.

Aidan and Roarke stepped up behind Cass and Del, putting

their hands on their shoulders. It was clear—they would come as well. And they were good allies. We had loads of good allies.

If it didn't go in our favor tomorrow—we'd fight our way out. Then we'd start again.

But I really didn't want to start again.

~

The next morning, the six of us stood in the waiting room of the council chambers. I'd never been to the Order of the Magica headquarters. Hell, none of us had ever been here.

We avoided this massive brick building like the plague, living our whole lives under the radar. Even Del, who worked part-time as a mercenary, had avoided this building and worked solely through intermediaries.

But here we were, in the fancy waiting room done in gleaming wood and gold. When we'd walked across the court-yard twenty minutes ago, I'd seen friends loitering on benches and leaning against trees.

Connor and Claire sat on the hood of a car, Aerdeca and Mordaca on a bench. My parents at a cafe. Pond Flower with Emile, her keen gaze on us. Quite a few vampires were there as well—even Doyen and Magisteria, though they waited in the deep shadows of trees to avoid the sun. Even Jeff sat in an oak tree, small and hidden in the leaves.

They all waited as backup, in case this went south.

We had friends. Help. Always.

I drew in a shuddering breath, my gaze riveted to the door to the main chamber. It was an ornate wooden affair, screaming wealth and power. We'd never had much use for the Order other than to avoid them. I appreciated that they kept law and order, but I didn't want them keeping it with *us*.

Ares squeezed my hand, a silent gesture that we'd get out of this intact.

"It'll be all right," Aidan said.

"You know that?" I asked him. He had contacts here. Maybe...

"No. But have faith."

I nodded, meeting Cass and Del's eyes. We'd flown under the radar for so long. *Please don't let this be the end.*

Finally, after a decade of waiting, the door creaked open. A slender young man dressed in a somber black suit stepped out. "It is time."

We followed him in, my heart in my throat.

Somehow, this was more frightening than facing Drakon and his army. These people could take my whole life from me. It was somehow more real than my own death. Hell, I'd come back from my own death. But I couldn't rebuild this life in Magic's Bend.

The main chamber was a large, rectangular room. A massive, glittering chandelier shed light on the long table in front of us. Seven figures sat behind it, four men and three women. Each was dressed somberly, their faces stern.

In front of them was a row of six chairs. Like the principal's office, but on steroids. We approached, stopping behind the chairs.

An older, white-haired gentleman stood. His dark gaze was hard, his face devoid of pleasantness or levity. He gestured to the six chairs.

Suddenly, I was annoyed. My fear was drowned out by disbelief.

"You've got to be kidding, right?" I said.

No way I was sitting in one of those little chairs. Whatever they were going to throw at us—it was coming. But damned if I'd sit in the naughty kids' chair only days after I'd thrown myself to my death to save the world.

The man coughed and shifted, suddenly uncomfortable. "Yes, yes. Clearly that was a poor idea."

Confusion flared. Yeah, *I* knew that had been a shit idea. But that he agreed?

"We are creatures of tradition here, you see," he said.

"And tradition is to try to make everyone who visits seem small?" Cass asked.

Del made a *tsk*ing noise. "It's an old trick. And not a very good one."

As much as I was scared witless of what these people knew about me, I wasn't about to play their games. I'd faced worse than them, no matter how much control they might have over my life and booting me from the home I loved. While I was terrified of that outcome, I couldn't bear to bow to them.

Not after everything that had happened.

"Ah." The Order leader hesitated, then seemed to catch himself. "Tradition," he boomed.

Tradition was them harping on their own power while being afraid of everyone else's, but whatever. I stood silently, waiting for him to get it over with.

"Tradition says that FireSouls are evil," he continued.

Shit.

"But we may have been wrong."

My brows arched.

"We've had our suspicions for some time about you three." He shifted. "At first, you seemed weak. Normal. But over the last year, we have noticed that your power has grown. Quite substantially, according to our sources."

Their sources had to be the mercenaries that they'd sent to help us fight impossible battles. It'd been a risk to solicit their assistance, but it'd been necessary. We hadn't been willing to risk the safety of the world to save our own hides.

Apparently that was biting us in the ass now.

"What is it you're trying to say?" I asked.

The woman next to him stood. "What we're trying to say is, thank you."

"Thank you?" Shock dropped my jaw.

"Yes. We've pieced together a bit of what you've done. Not a lot, but enough that we realize we must change our ways. Therefore, we are pardoning you."

"Pardoning us? From being what we are?" I appreciated that I wasn't in trouble—but the wording was crap. "We saved your asses. There's nothing wrong with FireSouls."

"Get 'em," Cass whispered.

"We see that now. Mostly." The woman's face firmed. "We thank you for what you've done—saving the dragons, and us. Our fear led to prejudice, and that was unfair to you. We recognize that now."

"What about other FireSouls? Are they safe from you?" I thought of the League of FireSouls. They'd made as many sacrifices as we had.

The solemn figures behind the table hesitated. Finally, the man spoke. "We cannot guarantee anything. Change is slow to come. Rest assured that you are safe. As for the others, we will be more lenient with them."

"Good." I frowned at them all. "Because they saved you too."

"We must be wary of power unchecked," the man blustered. "Balance is key. Balance is safe. It is our job to ensure it lasts."

The woman stepped forward. "But we will try. Be assured of that."

It was clearly the best that we would get out of them. I nodded, then turned. It was time to get the hell out of here. There wasn't much left to say anyway.

We walked out of the room as a group. The back of my neck burned all the way to the main door, but the air outside was sweet.

We were free.

As the heavy wooden door slammed behind us, I turned to Cass and Del.

"That's it." I laughed.

"I can't believe that just happened," Del said. "We don't have to be afraid of them anymore."

"No more hiding," Cass said. "No more running."

"What were they going to do to you anyway?" Ares said. "Nix came back from the dead. The three of you are all more powerful than everyone in there. You have allies everywhere. They can no longer touch you."

"It was a smart move on their part," Aidan said.

"They didn't have much choice," Roarke added.

"You're right. But still…" I thought back to their faces. "I do think they were truly grateful to us."

"They were," Cass said. "And after the sacrifices we've made, it's clear we mean them no harm. Their stupid prejudice is crumbling."

"We made that happen," Del said. "And it'll keep crumbling. They're afraid, but they'll have to get over it."

"I think they will." I hugged my *deirfiúr*, memories of our pasts racing through my mind. We'd been through so much, good and bad. And we'd come out the other end. The world was a better place. And I was here with them now, safe. All of us were safe. And the whole world was ahead of us.

∿

Ares and I sat on the hillside overlooking my village below. All around us, grass bloomed in profusion. The trees sprouted buds, and flowers grew along the streams. I'd even seen the forest spirit, who was looking much more substantial lately.

Down below in the village, people sang and danced. In the distance, Jeff flew through the fields, blowing the petals off daisies, occasionally burning them with his fire by accident.

Elesius was recovering. Growing again. The magic that I'd given the forest spirit had jumpstarted the process. And now life was finding a way.

I snickered quietly at the *Jurassic Park* reference, then leaned against Ares, absorbing his warmth. "I'm so glad there weren't many casualties."

"I'm glad that I didn't lose who I cherish most." He wrapped an arm around me and squeezed. "Your plan was a good one. Waiting for the dragons saved all the fighters. As a team, they were victorious. But you... You risked your life. Died for your cause."

"I had to. There was no other way." I smiled. "And it's hard to lose a battle with three dragons on your side." I thought back to the fight. "And the demons were fighting for a shitty reason. Our side, however ... They were fighting for something real."

"No kidding." Ares kissed my head. "And they had a good leader."

I grinned up at him. "Not me. I was hardly there at all. That battle was a team effort. Everything we've done is a team effort. I was busy throwing myself into a pit."

He shuddered, pulling me close. "I should have realized you'd do that."

"I'm just lucky I came back." I smiled.

"Phoenix. Your name is apt. And I'm grateful I fell in love with a woman who can come back from the dead." He shuddered. "I can't bear to think of the alternative."

"I wonder if my mother knew I'd come back?" Though Cass, Del, and I had thought we'd named ourselves for the stars above when we'd woken in that field with no memory. We'd been wrong. My mother had given me that name, and I'd remembered.

"I think she may have," Ares said. "She's a stoic woman, committed to duty. But she's committed to you above all."

I nodded. "And this whole time, when she spoke of sacrifice and doing our duty ... That would have been terrible if she'd thought I'd die. That we'd all die."

"Exactly. So I think she may have known. Or sensed. Or hoped."

"Whatever the case, I'm glad it worked out." I played with the grass at my side. "And now Elesius can grow again. And thrive."

"No more battles."

"No more war." I turned to him and kissed him. "I'm glad I found you. And that I have a life left to enjoy with you."

"Your whole life?" The corner of Ares's mouth tugged up.

"I was thinking maybe, yeah. Give it a try."

"Good. I was thinking the same. I've lost you once. I don't plan to lose you again." He pulled me close and kissed me hard, his mouth warm and skilled.

I wrapped my arms around him and sank into the kiss. After a moment, I pulled away. "I'm glad we're fated. It feels right."

"Even if it weren't fated, I'd make it so. I want to spend my life with you, Nix."

"Likewise." I looked down at the valley below. "I can't believe how lucky I am. I found you. My *deirfiúr* and I are alive. We get to have our home in Magic's Bend. Even Elesius is thriving."

"Lucky, maybe." Ares squeezed my hand. "But I think a person makes their own luck. And Nix—you've definitely made your own luck."

I looked at him and smiled. "I want to keep making it."

"You will."

I kissed him again, then turned my gaze back to my town. I leaned against him, enjoying the view. It still amazed me—everything that I had. We'd have dinner with my parents later, then go back to Magic's Bend and have drinks with Cass and Del.

This was my future. I'd made it through the dark part and arrived, along with everyone I loved. I couldn't wait to see what was next.

~~~

Thank you for reading! If you haven't read *Hidden Magic*, the story of how the FireSouls got into the magic hunting business, you can join my mailing list and get it for free. Bree and Ana's adventure is about to start. Turn the page for an excerpt.

THANK YOU FOR READING!

I hope you enjoyed Nix's series as much as I enjoyed writing it. Reviews are *so* helpful to authors. I really appreciate all reviews, both positive and negative. If you want to leave one, you can do so on Amazon or GoodReads.

For now, the Dragon's Gift series is complete. But the adventures aren't over. If you haven't read Cass's or Del's series, you can find them on Amazon. Or, if you liked Bree and Ana, they will have a series coming out later this year. Join my mailing list at www.linseyhall.com/subscribe to stay updated.

EXCERPT OF HIDDEN MAGIC

Jungle, Southeast Asia
   Five years before the events in Ancient Magic

"How much are we being paid for this job again?" I glanced at the dudes filling the bar. It was a motley crowd of supernaturals, many of whom looked shifty as hell.

"Not nearly enough for one as dangerous as this." Del frowned at the man across the bar, who was giving her his best sexy face. There was a lot of eyebrow movement happening. "Is he having a seizure?"

"Looks like it." Nix grinned. "Though I gotta say, I wasn't expecting this. We're basically in a tree, for magic's sake. In the middle of the jungle! Where are all these dudes coming from?"

"According to my info, there's a mining operation near here. Though I'd say we're more *under* a tree than *in* a tree."

"I'm with Cass," Del said. "Under, not in."

"Fair enough," Nix said.

We were deep in Southeast Asia, in a bar that had long ago been reclaimed by the jungle. A massive fig tree had grown over and around the ancient building, its huge roots strangling the stone walls. It was straight out of a fairy tale.

Monks had once lived here, but a few supernaturals of indeterminate species had gotten ahold of it and turned it into a watering hole for the local supernaturals. We were meeting our contact here, but he was late.

"Hey, pretty lady." A smarmy voice sounded from my left. "What are you?"

I turned to face the guy who was giving me the up and down, his gaze roving from my tank top to my shorts. He wasn't Clarence, our local contact. And if he meant "what kind of supernatural are you?" I sure as hell wouldn't be answering. That could get me killed.

"Not interested is what I am," I said.

"Aww, that's no way to treat a guy." He grabbed my hip, rubbed his thumb up and down.

I smacked his hand away, tempted to throat-punch him. It was my favorite move, but I didn't want to start a fight before Clarence got here. Didn't want to piss off our boss.

The man raised his hands. "Hey, hey. No need to get feisty. You three sisters?"

I glanced at Nix and Del, at their dark hair that was so different from my red. We were all about twenty, but we looked nothing alike. And while we might call ourselves sisters—*deirfiúr* in our native Irish—this idiot didn't know that.

"Go away." I had no patience for dirt bags who touched me without asking. "Run along and flirt with your hand, because that's all the action you'll be getting tonight."

His face turned a mottled red, and he raised a fist. His magic welled, the scent of rotten fruit overwhelming.

He thought he was going to smack me? Or use his magic against me?

Ha.

I lashed out, punching him in the throat. His eyes bulged and he gagged. I kneed him in the crotch, grinning when he keeled over.

"Hey!" A burly man with a beard lunged for us, his buddy beside him following. "That's no way—"

"To treat a guy?" I finished for him as I kicked out at him. My tall, heavy boots collided with his chest, sending him flying backward. I never used my magic—didn't want to go to jail and didn't want to blow things up—but I sure as hell could fight.

His friend raised his hand and sent a blast of wind at us. It threw me backward, sending me skidding across the floor.

By the time I'd scrambled to my feet, a brawl had broken out in the bar. Fists flew left and right, with a bit of magic thrown in. Nothing bad enough to ruin the bar, like jets of flame, because no one wanted to destroy the only watering hole for a hundred miles, but enough that it lit up the air with varying magical signatures.

Nix conjured a baseball bat and swung it at a burly guy who charged her, while Del teleported behind a horned demon and smashed a chair over his head. I'd always been jealous of Del's ability to sneak up on people like that.

All in all, it was turning into a good evening. A fight between supernaturals was fun.

"Enough!" the bartender bellowed. "Or no more beer!"

The patrons quieted immediately. Fights might be fun, but they weren't worth losing beer over.

I glared at the jerk who'd started it. There was no way I'd take the blame, even though I'd thrown the first punch. He should have known better.

The bartender gave me a look and I shrugged, hiking a thumb at the jerk who'd touched me. "He shoulda kept his hands to himself."

"Fair enough," the bartender said.

I nodded and turned to find Nix and Del. They'd grabbed our

beers and were putting them on a table in the corner. I went to join them.

We were a team. Sisters by choice, ever since we'd woken in a field at fifteen with no memories other than those that said we were FireSouls on the run from someone who had hurt us. Who was hunting us.

Our biggest goal, even bigger than getting out from under our current boss's thumb, was to save enough money to buy concealment charms that would hide us from the monster who hunted us. He was just a shadowy memory, but it was enough to keep us running.

"Where is Clarence, anyway?" I pulled my damp tank top away from my sweaty skin. The jungle was damned hot. We couldn't break into the temple until Clarence gave us the information we needed to get past the guard at the front. And we didn't need to spend too much longer in this bar.

Del glanced at her watch, her blue eyes flashing with annoyance. "He's twenty minutes late. Old Man Bastard said he should be here at eight."

Old Man Bastard—OMB for short—was our boss. His name said it all. Del, Nix, and I were FireSouls, the most despised species of supernatural because we could steal other magical being's powers if we killed them. We'd never done that, of course, but OMB didn't care. He'd figured out our secret when we were too young to hide it effectively and had been blackmailing us to work for him ever since.

It'd been four years of finding and stealing treasure on his behalf. Treasure hunting was our other talent, a gift from the dragon with whom legend said we shared a soul. No one had seen a dragon in centuries, so I wasn't sure if the legend was even true, but dragons were covetous, so it made sense they had a knack for finding treasure.

"What are we after again?" Nix asked.

"A pair of obsidian daggers," Del said. "Nice ones."

"And how much is this job worth?" Nix repeated my earlier question. Money was always on our minds. It was our only chance at buying our freedom, but OMB didn't pay us enough for it to be feasible anytime soon. We kept meticulous track of our earnings and saved like misers anyway.

"A thousand each."

"Damn, that's pathetic." I slouched back in my chair and stared up at the ceiling, too bummed about our crappy pay to even be impressed by the stonework and vines above my head.

"Hey, pretty ladies." The oily voice made my skin crawl. We just couldn't get a break in here. I looked up to see Clarence, our contact.

Clarence was a tall man, slender as a vine, and had the slicked back hair and pencil-thin mustache of a 1940s movie star. Unfortunately, it didn't work on him. Probably because his stare was like a lizard's. He was more Gomez Addams than Clark Gable. I'd bet anything that he liked working for OMB.

"Hey, Clarence," I said. "Pull up a seat and tell us how to get into the temple."

Clarence slid into a chair, his movement eerily snakelike. I shivered and scooted my chair away, bumping into Del. The scent of her magic flared, a clean hit of fresh laundry, as she no doubt suppressed her instinct to transport away from Clarence. If I had her gift of teleportation, I'd have to repress it as well.

"How about a drink first?" Clarence said.

Del growled, but Nix interjected, her voice almost nice. She had the most self control out of the three of us. "No can do, Clarence. You know... Mr. Oribis"—her voice tripped on the name, probably because she wanted to call him OMB—"wants the daggers soon. Maybe next time, though."

"Next time." Clarence shook his head like he didn't believe her. He might be a snake, but he was a clever one. His chest puffed up a bit. "You know I'm the only one who knows how to get into the temple. How to get into any of the places in this jungle."

"And we're so grateful you're meeting with us. Mr. Oribis is so grateful." Nix dug into her pocket and pulled out the crumpled envelope that contained Clarence's pay. We'd counted it and found—unsurprisingly—that it was more than ours combined, even though all he had to do was chat with us for two minutes. I'd wanted to scream when I'd seen it.

Clarence's gaze snapped to the money. "All right, all right."

Apparently his need to be flattered went out the window when cash was in front of his face. Couldn't blame him, though. I was the same way.

"So, what are we up against?" I asked.

The temple containing the daggers had been built by supernaturals over a thousand years ago. Like other temples of its kind, it was magically protected. Clarence's intel would save us a ton of time and damage to the temple if we could get around the enchantments rather than breaking through them.

"Dvarapala. A big one."

"A gatekeeper?" I'd seen one of the giant, stone monster statues at another temple before.

"Yep." He nodded slowly. "Impossible to get through. The temple's as big as the Titanic—hidden from humans, of course—but no one's been inside in centuries, they say."

Hidden from humans was a given. They had no idea supernaturals existed, and we wanted to keep it that way.

"So how'd you figure out the way in?" Del asked. "And why *haven't* you gone in? Bet there's lots of stuff you could fence in there. Temples are usually full of treasure."

"A bit of pertinent research told me how to get in. And I'd rather sell the entrance information and save my hide. It won't be easy to get past the booby traps in there."

Hide? Snakeskin, more like. Though he had a point. I didn't think he'd last long trying to get through a temple on his own.

"So? Spill it," I said, anxious to get going.

He leaned in, and the overpowering scent of cologne and sweat hit me. I grimaced, held my breath, then leaned forward to hear his whispers.

~

As soon as Clarence walked away, the communications charms around my neck vibrated. I jumped, then groaned. Only one person had access to this charm.

I shoved the small package Clarence had given me into my short's pocket and pressed my fingertips to the comms charm, igniting its magic.

"Hello, Mr. Oribis." I swallowed my bile at having to be polite.

"Girls," he grumbled.

Nix made a gagging face. We hated when he called us girls.

"Change of plans. You need to go to the temple tonight."

"What? But it's dark. We're going tomorrow." He never changed the plans on us. This was weird.

"I need the daggers sooner. Go tonight."

My mind raced. "The jungle is more dangerous in the dark. We'll do it if you pay us more."

"Twice the usual," Del said.

A tinny laugh echoed from the charm. "Pay *you* more? You're lucky I pay you at all."

I gritted my teeth and said, "But we've been working for you for four years without a raise."

"And you'll be working for me for four more years. And four after that. And four after that." Annoyance lurked in his tone. So did his low opinion of us.

Del's and Nix's brows crinkled in distress. We'd always suspected that OMB wasn't planning to let us buy our freedom, but he'd dangled that carrot in front of us. What he'd just said made that seem like a big fat lie, though. One we could add to the many others he'd told us.

An urge to rebel, to stand up to the bully who controlled our lives, seethed in my chest.

"No," I said. "You treat us like crap, and I'm sick of it. Pay us fairly."

"I treat you like *crap*, as you so eloquently put it, because that is exactly what you are. *FireSouls*." He spit the last word, imbuing it with so much venom I thought it might poison me.

I flinched, frantically glancing around to see if anyone in the bar had heard what he'd called us. Fortunately, they were all distracted. That didn't stop my heart from thundering in my ears as rage replaced the fear. I opened my mouth to shout at him, but snapped it shut. I was too afraid of pissing him off.

"Get it by dawn," he barked. "Or I'm turning one of you in to the Order of the Magica. Prison will be the least of your worries. They might just execute you."

I gasped. "You wouldn't." Our government hunted and imprisoned—or destroyed—FireSouls.

"Oh, I would. And I'd enjoy it. The three of you have been more trouble than you're worth. You're getting cocky, thinking you have a say in things like this. Get the daggers by dawn, or one of you ends up in the hands of the Order."

My skin chilled, and the floor felt like it had dropped out from under me. He was serious.

"Fine." I bit off the end of the word, barely keeping my voice from shaking. "We'll do it tonight. Del will transport them to you as soon as we have them."

"Excellent." Satisfaction rang in his tone, and my skin crawled. "Don't disappoint me, or you know what will happen."

The magic in the charm died. He'd broken the connection.

I collapsed back against the chair. In times like these, I wished I had it in me to kill. Sure, I offed demons when they came at me on our jobs, but that was easy because they didn't actually die. Killing their earthly bodies just sent them back to their hell.

But I couldn't kill another supernatural. Not even OMB. It might get us out of this lifetime of servitude, but I didn't have it in me. And what if I failed? I was too afraid of his rage—and the consequences—if I didn't succeed.

"Shit, shit, shit." Nix's green eyes were stark in her pale face. "He means it."

"Yeah." Del's voice shook. "We need to get those daggers."

"Now," I said.

"I wish I could just conjure a forgery," Nix said. "I really don't want to go out into the jungle tonight. Getting past the Dvarapala in the dark will suck."

Nix was a conjurer, able to create almost anything using just her magic. Massive or complex things, like airplanes or guns, were outside of her ability, but a couple of daggers wouldn't be hard.

Trouble was, they were a magical artifact, enchanted with the ability to return to whoever had thrown them. Like boomerangs. Though Nix could conjure the daggers, we couldn't enchant them.

"We need to go. We only have six hours until dawn." I grabbed my short swords from the table and stood, shoving them into the holsters strapped to my back.

A hush descended over the crowded bar.

I stiffened, but the sound of the staticky TV in the corner made me relax. They weren't interested in me. Just the news, which was probably being routed through a dozen techno-witches to get this far into the jungle.

The grave voice of the female reporter echoed through the quiet bar. "The FireSoul was apprehended outside of his apartment in Magic's Bend, Oregon. He is currently in the custody of the Order of the Magica, and his trial is scheduled for tomorrow morning. My sources report that execution is possible."

I stifled a crazed laugh. Perfect timing. Just what we needed to hear after OMB's threat. A reminder of what would happen if he turned us into the Order of the Magica. The hush that had descended over the previously rowdy crowd—the kind of hush you get at the scene of a big accident—indicated what an interesting freaking topic this was. FireSouls were the bogeymen. *I* was the bogeyman, even though I didn't use my powers. But as long as no one found out, we were safe.

My gaze darted to Del and Nix. They nodded toward the door. It was definitely time to go.

As the newscaster turned her report toward something more boring and the crowd got rowdy again, we threaded our way between the tiny tables and chairs.

I shoved the heavy wooden door open and sucked in a breath of sticky jungle air, relieved to be out of the bar. Night creatures screeched, and moonlight filtered through the trees above. The jungle would be a nice place if it weren't full of things that wanted to kill us.

"We're never escaping him, are we?" Nix said softly.

"We will." Somehow. Someday. "Let's just deal with this for now."

We found our motorcycles, which were parked in the lot with a dozen other identical ones. They were hulking beasts with massive, all-terrain tires meant for the jungle floor. We'd done a lot of work in Southeast Asia this year, and these were our favored forms of transportation in this part of the world.

Del could transport us, but it was better if she saved her power. It wasn't infinite, though it did regenerate. But we'd learned a long time ago to save Del's power for our escape. Nothing worse than being trapped in a temple with pissed off guardians and a few tripped booby traps.

We'd scouted out the location of the temple earlier that day, so we knew where to go.

I swung my leg over Secretariat—I liked to name my vehicles

—and kicked the clutch. The engine roared to life. Nix and Del followed, and we peeled out of the lot, leaving the dingy yellow light of the bar behind.

Our headlights illuminated the dirt road as we sped through the night. Huge fig trees dotted the path on either side, their twisted trunks and roots forming an eerie corridor. Elephant-ear sized leaves swayed in the wind, a dark emerald that gleamed in the light.

Jungle animals howled, and enormous lightning bugs flitted along the path. They were too big to be regular bugs, so they were most likely some kind of fairy, but I wasn't going to stop to investigate. There were dangerous creatures in the jungle at night —one of the reasons we hadn't wanted to go now—and in our world, fairies could be considered dangerous.

Especially if you called them lightning bugs.

A roar sounded in the distance, echoing through the jungle and making the leaves rustle on either side as small animals scurried for safety.

The roar came again, only closer.

Then another, and another.

"Oh shit," I muttered. This was bad.

~~~

Join my mailing list at www.linseyhallauthor.com/subscribe to get a free copy ebook copy of *Hidden Magic*. No spam and you can leave anytime!

AUTHOR'S NOTE

Thank you so much for reading *Forged in Magic!* If you're interested in learning more about the historical elements in this book, read on. At the end, I'll talk a bit about why Nix and her *deirfiúr* are treasure hunters and how I try to make that fit with archaeology's ethics (which don't condone treasure hunting, as I'm sure you might have guessed).

Forged in Magic had several historical and mythological influences. The most obvious are the Greek myths in Nix's first challenge. While I invented the mini-realms of each of the Greek gods, the characteristics of those realms borrowed directly from mythology. While Nestor the Twinkie loving sea turtle and the Stone of Synnaroe were pure fabrication, most of the rest was not. Some of my favorites that were taken directly from myth were Hades's invisibility helmet, the river Acheron, Athena's owl, and the Empusa.

The story of Medusa that I chose to use was from the Roman poet Ovid. There are actually a couple of versions of Medusa's creation—I chose the one that gave Nix a morality test.

The primordial gods on Svalbard were invention, but the boat of the gods that took them to Svalbard was not. Skithblathnir was supposed to be the best of the ships in Norse Mythology. In mythology, it could be filed up and stored in the pocket. Snorri Sturluson wrote about the boat in his Prose Edda and Heimskringla. As I mentioned in the book, Snorri was a poet and historian in 13th century Iceland. For the departure point to Svalbard, I chose the name Heimskringla as a tribute to his work.

That's it for the historical influences in *Forged in Magic.* However, one of the most important things about this book is how Nix and her *deirfiúr* treat artifacts and their business, Ancient Magic.

As I'm sure you know, archaeology isn't quite like Indiana Jones (for which I'm both grateful and bitterly disappointed). Sure, it's exciting and full of travel. However, booby-traps are not as common as I expected. Total number of booby-traps I have encountered in my career: zero. Still hoping, though.

When I chose to write a series about archaeology and treasure hunting, I knew I had a careful line to tread. There is a big difference between these two activities. As much as I value artifacts, they are not treasure. Not even the gold artifacts. They are pieces of our history that contain valuable information, and as such, they belong to all of us. Every artifact that is excavated should be properly conserved and stored in a museum so that everyone can have access to our history. No one single person can own history, and I believe very strongly that individuals should not own artifacts. Treasure hunting is the pursuit of artifacts for personal gain.

So why did I make Nix and her *deirfiúr* treasure hunters? I'd have loved to call them archaeologists, but nothing about their work is like archaeology. Archaeology is a very laborious, painstaking process—and it certainly doesn't involve selling artifacts. That wouldn't work for the fast-paced, adventurous series that I had planned for *Dragon's Gift.* Not to mention the fact that dragons are famous for coveting treasure. Considering where the *deirfiúr* got their skills from, it just made sense to call them treasure hunters.

Even though I write urban fantasy, I strive for accuracy. The *deirfiúr* don't engage in archaeological practices—therefore, I cannot call them archaeologists. I also have a duty as an archaeologist to properly represent my field and our goals—namely, to protect and share history. Treasure hunting doesn't do this. One of the biggest battles that archaeology faces today is protecting cultural heritage from thieves.

I debated long and hard about not only what to call the heroines of this series, but also about how they would do their jobs. I wanted it to involve all the cool things we think about when we think about archaeology—namely, the Indiana Jones stuff, whether it's real or not. But I didn't know quite how to do that while still staying within the bounds of my own ethics. I can cut myself and other writers some slack because this is fiction, but I couldn't go too far into smash and grab treasure hunting.

I consulted some of my archaeology colleagues to get their take, which was immensely helpful. Wayne Lusardi, the State Maritime Archaeologist for Michigan, and Douglas Inglis and Veronica Morris, both archaeologists for Interactive Heritage, were immensely helpful with ideas. My biggest problem was figuring out how to have the heroines steal artifacts from tombs and then sell them and still sleep at night. Everything I've just said is pretty counter to this, right?

That's where the magic comes in. The heroines aren't after the artifacts themselves (they put them back where they found them, if you recall)—they're after the magic that the artifacts contain. They're more like magic hunters than treasure hunters. That solved a big part of my problem. At least they were putting the artifacts back. Though that's not proper archaeology, I could let it pass. At least it's clear that they believe they shouldn't keep the artifact or harm the site. But the SuperNerd in me said, "Well, that magic is part of the artifact's context. It's important to the artifact and shouldn't be removed and sold."

Now *that* was a problem. I couldn't escape my SuperNerd self, so I was in a real conundrum. Fortunately, that's where the immensely intelligent Wayne Lusardi came in. He suggested that the magic could have an expiration date. If the magic wasn't used before it decayed, it could cause huge problems. Think explosions and tornado spells run amok. It could ruin the entire site, not to mention possibly cause injury and death. That would be very bad.

So now you see why Nix and her *deirfiúr* don't just steal artifacts to sell them. Not only is selling the magic cooler, it's also better from an ethical standpoint, especially if the magic was going to cause problems in the long run. These aren't perfect solutions—the perfect solution would be sending in a team of archaeologists to carefully record the site and remove the dangerous magic—but that wouldn't be a very fun book.

Thanks again for reading (especially if you got this far!).

ACKNOWLEDGMENTS

Thank you, Ben, for everything. There would be no books without you.

Thank you to Jena O'Connor, Lindsey Loucks, and Donna Rich for your excellent editing. The book is immensely better because of you both! Thank you to Orina Kafe for the beautiful cover art. Thank you to Eleonora, Crystal Jeffs, Richard Goodrum, and Jessie Crosby for your keen eyes in spotting errors.

The Dragon's Gift series is a product of my two lives: one as an archaeologist and one as a novelist. Combining these two took a bit of work. I'd like to thank my friends, Wayne Lusardi, the State Maritime Archaeologist for Michigan, and Douglas Inglis and Veronica Morris, both archaeologists for Interactive Heritage, for their ideas about how to have a treasure hunter heroine that doesn't conflict too much with archaeology's ethics. The Author's Note contains a bit more about this if you are interested.

GLOSSARY

Alpha Council - There are two governments that enforce law for supernaturals—the Alpha Council and the Order of the Magica. The Alpha Council governs all shifters. They work cooperatively with the Alpha Council when necessary—for example, when capturing FireSouls.

Blood Sorceress - A type of Magica who can create magic using blood.

Conjurer - A Magica who uses magic to create something from nothing. They cannot create magic, but if there is magic around them, they can put that magic into their conjuration.

Dark Magic - The kind that is meant to harm. It's not necessarily bad, but it often is.

Deirfiúr - Sisters in Irish.

Demons - Often employed to do evil. They live in various hells but can be released upon the earth if you know how to get to them and then get them out. If they are killed on Earth, they are sent back to their hell.

Dragon Sense - A FireSoul's ability to find treasure. It is an internal sense that pulls them toward what they seek. It is easiest to find gold, but they can find anything or anyone that is valued by someone.

Elemental Mage – A rare type of mage who can manipulate all of the elements.

Enchanted Artifacts – Artifacts can be imbued with magic that lasts after the death of the person who put the magic into the artifact (unlike a spell that has not been put into an artifact—these spells disappear after the Magica's death). But magic is not stable. After a period of time—hundreds or thousands of years depending on the circumstance—the magic will degrade. Eventually, it can go bad and cause many problems.

Fire Mage – A mage who can control fire.

FireSoul - A very rare type of Magica who shares a piece of the dragon's soul. They can locate treasure and steal the gifts (powers) of other supernaturals. With practice, they can manipulate the gifts they steal, becoming the strongest of that gift. They are despised and feared. If they are caught, they are thrown in the Prison of Magical Deviants.

The Great Peace - The most powerful piece of magic ever created. It hides magic from the eyes of humans.

Hearth Witch – A Magica who is versed in magic relating to hearth and home. They are often good at potions and protective spells and are also very perceptive when on their own turf.

Informa - A supernatural who can steal powers.

Magica - Any supernatural who has the power to create magic —witches, sorcerers, mages. All are governed by the Order of the Magica.

The Origin - The descendent of the original alpha shifter. They are the most powerful shifter and can turn into any species.

Order of the Magica - There are two governments that enforce law for supernaturals—the Alpha Council and the Order of the Magica. The Order of the Magica govern all Magica. They work cooperatively with the Alpha Council when necessary—for example, when capturing FireSouls.

Phantom - A type of supernatural that is similar to a ghost. They are incorporeal. They feed off the misery and pain of others, forcing them to relive their greatest nightmares and fears. They do not have a fully functioning mind like a human or supernatural. Rather, they are a shadow of their former selves. Half-bloods are extraordinarily rare.

Seeker - A type of supernatural who can find things. FireSouls often pass off their dragon sense as Seeker power.

Shifter - A supernatural who can turn into an animal. All are governed by the Alpha Council.

Transporter - A type of supernatural who can travel anywhere. Their power is limited and must regenerate after each use.

Vampire - Blood drinking supernaturals with great strength and speed who live in a separate realm.

Warden of the Underworld - A one of a kind position created by Roarke. He keeps order in the Underworld.

ABOUT LINSEY

Before becoming a writer, Linsey Hall was a nautical archaeologist who studied shipwrecks from Hawaii and the Yukon to the UK and the Mediterranean. She credits fantasy and historical romances with her love of history and her career as an archaeologist. After a decade of tromping around the globe in search of old bits of stuff that people left lying about, she settled down and started penning her own romance novels. Her Dragon's Gift series draws upon her love of history and the paranormal elements that she can't help but include.

COPYRIGHT

Made in the USA
Columbia, SC
14 October 2018